The Body at Penford Priory

*

The Lady Jane & Mrs Forbes Mysteries

Book Three

B. D. CHURSTON

ISBN: 9798869801807

One

September 1928

Kate Forbes was driving Gertie, her cherry red Austin Seven, through the sunny Sussex countryside. In a cheerful mood, and amid all this marvellous scenery, she was wondering what might make the perfect weekend.

Obviously, seeing her niece, Lady Jane Scott again would be part of it. That was the reason for her Saturday morning journey to an ancient ruin. But what else?

Finding a body?

Yes, that would do it.

Just ahead, black lettering on a white sign indicated a crossroads junction. To the left was Upton. To the right, Mortimer Hall. However, her destination was straight ahead – the village of Penford. Only, she was brought to a halt by a flock of junction-blocking sheep.

Kate was in no hurry though. Indeed, it was an opportunity to take in the fields dotted with hay bales, the smiling young shepherdess and her border collie doing their best, and over to the right, a magnificent ancient stone edifice with nothing else attached to it. The priory ruin – once an important presence in these parts, but not for a very long time.

She knew all about Henry the Eighth, of course – the king who closed the monasteries. But all these centuries later, what might Jane and the archaeology team discover at the site?

While a 1908 effort failed to find anything, there was renewed optimism for this latest dig. A lot more research had been carried out. Fresh theories abounded. Not only would Jane and her colleagues find evidence of medieval life, they would also locate the final resting place of a 14th century prior named Wilfred.

At least, that was the hope.

So, yes, finding a body would be great, as long as no one expected Kate Forbes at fifty-three years of age to lend a hand with the digging.

That aside, perhaps she could be an assistant to Jane's boss, Professor Peregrine Nash, holding his tools or something. Or she could do a bit of work herself, poking around with a trowel, sort of thing.

Although…

What if she discovered the actual remains? Would that spoil things for the professor?

She could imagine the newspaper report.

The long-lost remains of Prior Wilfred were discovered by Mrs Kate Forbes within a few minutes of her very first attempt at digging. Archaeological expert, Professor Nash of Oxford University, who held a lifelong ambition to find the 14th century prior, was overcome with emotion.'

She didn't suppose Professor Nash would shake her by the hand. By the throat, perhaps.

"Ah, progress…"

With the last of the sheep coaxed off the road and into a field, Kate traversed the crossroads and continued past allotments which no doubt provided food for the blacksmiths, carpenters, wheelwrights, saddlers and others who served the district's farmers. Annoyingly though, someone was using their tiny plot to burn half the county's rubbish, turning the warm air acrid, and spoiling for a moment the perfection of the scene.

Passing a hay wagon, Kate entered the eastern end of Priory Street, which ran through the middle of Penford village.

This was home to a police house, a grocer's, the White Horse Inn, the post and telegraph office, the village green with its cricket pitch and boundary oak trees, St Peter's Church, a school, the Royal Oak pub, the Women's Institute hut, and the village dairy. Sitting among and around these landmarks were hundreds of whitewashed thatched cottages with gardens full of late summer blooms and fruits.

Kate steered Gertie onto a cobbled area at the side of the White Horse Inn, where hooves and carriage wheels had once clattered. It was a sizeable establishment with a dozen rooms for guests and would have been a prominent stop-off point for horse-drawn stagecoaches before the railways took over.

Here, Kate had booked a room for two nights. Not that there was much choice. The White Horse was the only decent place to stay, unless one was invited to sojourn at Mortimer Hall, which she hadn't been – unlike Jane who had mysteriously declined an invitation despite being an old schoolfriend of Lord Mortimer's granddaughter, Ursula Camley.

Having pulled up alongside Jane's burgundy and black Triumph Super Seven, Kate gave thanks for another long journey completed successfully. A few moments later, with a heavy suitcase in hand, she headed for the inn's side door, where a grey-haired local worker dashed forward to hold it open for her.

"Might you be Mrs Forbes?" he asked, his country accent being… not quite country.

She stared at him for a moment. His soft pale blue shirt was high quality cotton.

"Ah, you're the landlord."

"Not quite…"

"Aunt Kate!" A familiar figure appeared from inside wearing an army green blouse and dark green trousers.

"Jane!"

When Spanish Flu took Jane's mother, Annette, in 1919, Kate had tried to help her niece in any way she could. Annette had been Kate's younger sister and, nine years on, that desire to help was undiminished. Hence Kate wanting to wrap her arms around her niece, to ask if she was eating well, if she was happy, if… but aunts didn't do that sort of thing in public, which was a pity.

"I see you've met Professor Nash," said Jane.

"Ah…," said Kate, eyeing him once again – a man roughly her own age? "We haven't quite been introduced."

"Perry Nash, at your service," said the professor with a smile.

"And this is my aunt, Mrs Kate Forbes, as described," said Jane.

Kate tensed up a little.

"As described?"

"Described impeccably," said the professor. "Your niece suggested a woman of great dignity, a woman in her prime… What was the other thing, Jane?"

"The best aunt a girl could have."

"Oh, well…" Kate felt her face flush, but it wouldn't have shown due to Jane wrapping her arms around her and giving her a big hug.

"Mrs Forbes?" It was another arrival from within – a jolly man in his mid-forties with wavy black hair that had begun its journey towards silver. "Will Jessup, landlord. I'm sorry I wasn't out to greet you right away. I was watering the garden. May I take your case?"

"Oh, thank you, landlord. Most kind."

"I'll pop it into your room. Number Three, that is."

As he disappeared, Kate found herself gazing at the professor once again.

"So, digging," she said, looking away from his warm, grey eyes. "Have you had any luck?"

"Not yet, but we've only had a day so far. Why don't you come to the site after lunch – see what's what."

"Wonderful," said Kate. "It all sounds very intriguing. Do you think you'll locate Prior Wilfred?"

"Ah well, the main thing is to learn more about the priory and its history, but yes, we hope so."

As she was shown inside by both Jane and the professor, Kate tried to balance the idea of enjoying a convivial weekend while looking for a body. It was the sort of thing she'd had a little too much experience of over the past year.

That said, Professor Nash seemed an interesting chap. Pleasant, agreeable, handsome, a widower...

Not that she was interested in that sort of thing.

Two

Having packed her things away, Kate looked around the room. For a former coaching inn, it was lovely, with a good bed, a spacious mahogany wardrobe, a whitewashed chest of drawers, a tiled fireplace, a patterned rug, a padded armchair, tasteful pale green curtains, and two electric lamps – thanks to electricity coming to Penford just that summer.

There was also a fine view from the window – not only of the large garden below with its sturdy wooden bench seats and tables, and freshly-watered shrubs in beds and tubs, but also of sunlit fields, the river and stone bridge, and a quarter of a mile away to her right, the imposing priory ruin.

"Lunch then," she told herself.

The stairs descended directly into the inn's first-class lounge, giving Kate the opportunity to pause halfway down to take it all in.

It was a spacious area with a high ceiling and plenty of light from several large windows. Its walls featured brightly painted wagon wheels of varying sizes and, by the bar, wide black leather straps to which a variety of polished brass plaques were fixed – the sort of decoration one normally saw on a ceremonial horse harness. There were also a few large oil paintings of horse-drawn stagecoaches that drove home the inn's history.

Around the edges of the lounge, oak tables and high back chairs with floral cushions looked just the thing for dining, while, facing Kate across the room, a vast ornate mirror over the stone fireplace reflected her presence on the stairs.

To her left, two women were discussing something just outside the open double-door main entrance. To her right, Will Jessup was behind the beer taps chatting across the counter with a customer – an elderly chap on a stool at the wall end of the bar nursing the remains of a tankard of ale.

Finally, an archway at the far end on the right was signposted 'Public Lounge', which summoned up an image of plain décor and bare boards for agricultural workers coming in with muddy feet.

"Aunt Kate!" called Jane from a table between the fireplace and an open window.

Kate waved and came down to join her niece, nodding to the landlord on the way. Sitting with Jane were Professor Nash and a lean, handsome chap with a friendly face, warm brown eyes, and swept-back brown hair. He looked a similar age to Jane – who was twenty-seven.

Both men stood, while the younger of them came round to pull a chair out for her.

"Allow me…"

"Aunt Kate," said Jane, "meet my colleague, Harry Gibson."

"Pleased to meet you, Harry," said Kate.

"Mrs Forbes," he replied as she took her seat, "I've heard a lot about you. All good, of course, and some of it startlingly exciting."

"Oh… thank you."

Kate smiled as the men resumed their seats. Jane had clearly chosen a fine young chap to be her… friend.

"You've already met Professor Nash," said Jane.

"Please call me Perry," he insisted.

"Perry… then you must call me Kate."

"Kate…"

"Um… I must say I love the décor here, Perry. I'm often tempted to think like this at home."

Harry gasped. "A wagon wheel on the wall?"

"No, something of the seaside where I live. A ship's wheel perhaps. Or would that be too much, Jane?"

"Er… well… it's nice to respect the past. Look at this place. The White Horse must have been ever so busy in the old days."

"Well, Penford looks an ideal spot for walking and fishing. Perhaps Mr Jessup could advertise to get more motorists to come and stay."

"Did I hear my name?"

It was the landlord, Will Jessup, approaching with a smile.

"I was just saying I like the décor," said Kate.

"That's most kind, Mrs Forbes. I've tried to keep with tradition."

"Has the White Horse been in your family long?"

"Ah well," said Will. "My great-grandfather built it in 1845, but within ten years they put the railway through Upton. That was the end of the stagecoach, and unfortunately the White Horse suffered. Thankfully, we're doing just fine these days. Now what can I get you? We have fresh bread, butter, cheese, cold ham, eggs, fruit, honey…"

After a quick discussion, cheese and tomato sandwiches and glasses of cold lemonade were ordered.

"Those horse brasses," said Perry Nash, peering from the retreating landlord to the wall by the bar. "There's no shortage of history there." He glanced at Kate. "Then again, I'm sure you know as much as I do."

"Oh, I'm sure I don't, Perry. All I know is that they're brass plaques fixed onto a strap and used to decorate a horse."

"Yes, exactly – to decorate the harness gear, especially for shire and parade horses. It's fair to say their increasing popularity as a pub decoration correlates with the decline of horse-drawn transportation."

"Nostalgia," said Harry. "It's big business these days."

"Well, I'm all for it," said Kate. "These old coaching inns might be no more than ordinary pubs today, but it's good to remember the role they once played."

"Yes, absolutely," said Perry, "although we wouldn't want to tire you with endless talk of history."

"Nonsense," said Kate.

"We could talk for hours!" Harry warned.

"Good, I was hoping you'd tell me all about the priory."

"Ah…" said Perry. "A short version, perhaps. Harry's right. Having me going on and on would spoil lunch."

"I'm sure it wouldn't," said Kate. She studiously avoided Jane, who would no doubt be enjoying her aunt behaving like an awkward debutant.

"Yes, well," said Perry, "essentially, we're looking for evidence that helps us build a picture of life there before the Dissolution."

"What about Prior Wilfred?" Kate wondered.

"It would be terrific to find him. Certainly, in 1908, the vicar was particularly keen on it."

"Discussing the previous dig?" It was a question from a man in his fifties with a mustard three-piece suit, a greying moustache, thinning hair, and a commanding presence. He had just come in, no doubt bound for the bar, but he'd paused halfway across the floor.

"That's right," said Perry.

"Enright's the name. Aubrey Enright. The 1908 dig was a failure. More than thirty trenches and we found absolutely nothing. The vicar meant well, but him being in charge meant a lot of activity with little know-how. I was there making sure there was no funny business on Mortimer land. It's important to show the nobility that ordinary folk can be trustworthy."

"I was there too," said Perry. "Much younger then, of course. Peregrine Nash, at your service."

"Yes, I remember you. I'm on the parish council these days, but back then I was just a helping hand."

"Well, it's good to meet you again, Mr Enright."

"Yes, of course. Mind you, I have no interest in any of it now. Unlike yourself, I prefer to avoid the Mortimer estate."

Just then, Will Jessup arrived with their drinks on a tray.

"The sandwiches won't be long," he said.

"Weren't you on that first dig, Will?" the old chap at the bar wondered.

Will nodded. "I was! Mind you, I was a young man then, doing all kinds of work. They took me on as a hired hand, digging out those trenches for them. I can tell you it was no picnic."

"Enterprising," said Aubrey. "It's in our nature, see. I've done well in business myself. It's a new age. Men of merit working to improve the world. Not like the old money washing around uselessly among the woolly-headed old guard."

"I think he means the landed gentry," Jane whispered.

Aubrey huffed. "I'm just saying that by our enterprise, Penford's becoming self-sufficient."

"And what we can't get here, we can get in Upton," said the old chap.

"That wasn't my point," said Aubrey.

"Do not disturb the dead!" cried a woman at the open window.

Kate almost jumped out of her seat. The woman had appeared like an apparition, a notion not diminished by her long, gaunt visage and slender frame.

"Take no notice of Cecily," said the chap at the bar. "She likes to make a scene."

"I'm not making a scene, Sidney Allen. I'm merely stating a fact. No good will come of disturbing the dead. You mark my words."

Kate raised an eyebrow, while Jane addressed Cecily with a smile.

"If Prior Wilfred can be located, he'll be reburied in the church cemetery. I'm sure he'd approve."

"Who's to say it'll be the prior you dig up. You might unleash a presence to bring despair upon the village."

"I'm sure it won't come to that," said Kate, quite certain of it.

Three

Standing in a peaceful sunlit pasture, a quarter of a mile from the village and two hundred yards from Mortimer Hall, Kate and Perry Nash wore strikingly similar straw Panama hats which neither mentioned. All around them, wildflowers studded the short grass, tempting the occasional bee and butterfly, although the sheep or cattle responsible for all the munching had been moved elsewhere.

On one side of the expanse, dressed for field work and clearing the grass for a new trench, were Jane and a tall, blond student in a white shirt called Jeremy. Harry and a dark-haired, grey-shirted student, Owen, were on the other side. Owen and Jeremy looked no more than twenty.

"It's certainly an impressive front, if nothing else," said Kate, studying the impressive weather-worn ruin up close for the first time.

"It is," said Perry. "Just imagine it as an entire priory church. There would have also been dormitories with cells for the monks, a refectory, a gatehouse…"

"It must have been an inspiring presence for the parish."

"Ah, possibly not," said Perry. "Remember, it was a Cluniac priory."

"Cluniac?" Kate was lost entirely. Didn't cluniacs come out at night and howl at the moon?

"Why don't I get my students to enlighten you?" Perry suggested before summoning them.

All looked eager upon arrival.

"Let's help our guest with some information about the priory," said their leader.

Owen piped up. "There's a legend that says you can still hear the monks singing."

Jeremy nodded. "Apparently, the breeze carries their song."

Perry frowned. "Could we stick to history? I was telling Mrs Forbes this was a Cluniac establishment, but who were they exactly?"

Harry raised a hand.

"A monastic order dating back to the 11th century. Unlike the independent Benedictine monasteries, all Cluniac houses were part of a single institution under the control of Cluny Abbey."

"Cluny in France," Jeremy chimed in. "Burgundy, to be precise."

"That's right," said Owen. "In England, the Prior of Lewes ran the show under strict orders from the Abbot of Cluny."

"Very good," said Perry.

"Regarding Penford," said Harry. "The original Saxon church was dedicated to St. Martin of Tours. It was then rebuilt in 1148 to serve as a priory church... by which I mean it was for the use of monks only. That said, the de Vere family, as benefactors, are buried here."

"It all came to an end though," said Jeremy.

"Henry the Eighth," said Owen.

"Yes, he took possession of the priory here in 1538," said Harry. "Its destruction followed at the hands of Thomas Cromwell, the King's secretary."

"How fascinating," said Kate.

Perry smiled at his students' enthusiasm. "Yes, monasteries, priories, convents and friaries were disbanded so that their wealth might be used for the good of the people – which turned out to mean Henry spending it on himself and his military."

Harry nodded. "He sold the land here at Penford to the Earls of Dorset, who then sold it on. It eventually came to the Mortimers in 1772."

Kate looked around. In some ways, she felt a touch of sadness for the priory's destruction. She also felt a tinge of anger at the brutish King Henry.

"Let me show you our finds tent," Perry prompted.

They were soon outside a low apex canvas shelter with an open front. Inside were two seats at a table on which a dozen or so small items sat in a wooden tray.

"It's important to be able to study any finds we make," said Perry. "Shall we?"

Jane took their hats to facilitate their entry. Then, once seated, Kate was able to study at piece of mud-caked metal.

"This is nice," she said.

"Yes," said Perry. "We'll clean it up to see what's what, but it's clearly a belt buckle."

"From the mediaeval period?"

"More likely the Georgian period. Perhaps a worker who helped build the hall."

"Well, it's all incredibly fascinating," said Kate.

"Try this," said Perry, handing her a tiny piece of decorated pottery. "If you use your imagination, you can recreate the entire object in your mind."

Kate tried, and it turned into a teapot. She was thirsty...

Once they had exhausted the finds tray, they re-emerged into the sunlight where Jane handed them their hats. A moment later, an odd feeling over Kate's brow along with Jane's laughter hinted at a mix up. A glance at Perry, with an undersized Panama perched high on his head, confirmed it.

"Perhaps you should write your names in them," said Jane, still laughing.

Soon after, Kate and Perry strolled across to the old path.

"What became of it all?" Kate asked. "I mean physically. Apart from one edifice, it's disappeared completely."

"Not really," said Perry, pointing to Mortimer Hall, two hundred yards away.

"Oh, you don't mean...?"

"Ashlar stone from the priory."

"The thieves!"

"There's a gap between the 1540s and 1778, when the current hall was built. I'd guess an earlier hall was made of it and that too was cannibalised."

"How interesting."

"When you walk around the village, keep your eyes open for the stone in cottages, walls, St Peter's Church..."

"No..."

"Yes, indeed. It's a strange twist of fate, but part of St Peter's parish church was built with stone from the priory. You see, it never really disappeared. It was just reborn in a different form."

"How poetic, Perry."

"Oh, hardly, Kate."

She looked around again.

"So, tell me, what's the fascination with Wilfred?"

"Ah yes, Penford's most celebrated prior. He ran things for seventy years and lived to the grand old age of 102. We believe he was buried in the church in 1340, and then later reburied somewhere nearby."

"Almost six hundred years ago," Kate acknowledged.

"Yes," said Perry. "Jane found some de Vere family papers that mention Wilfred the Restless being relocated to a fitting plot. I think Wilfred was restless in that he regularly left the priory to spread the word among the locals. What if a fitting resting place was by the path to the gate?"

"Yes, why not," said Kate, thinking it made perfect sense.

"We believe he was laid to rest with a number of important artefacts. It won't be easy to find him, though – even with Jane's excellent research. The land turned to pasture centuries ago."

"Perhaps you'll be lucky."

"Yes… perhaps you could help us."

"Me?"

"Yes, Kate, would you like to dig?"

Kate tensed up. Digging was the last thing she wanted to do.

"Yes, of course, Perry. I've been itching to have a go."

"We'll start you with a new trench. That way, you'll see how the upper layers offer little unless someone dropped something in recent years. Once you've sifted some soil, we'll have the younger ones dig further and then get you back in. That way, you'll get to see first-hand how we roll back the years as we go deeper."

Kate was both relieved and interested.

"That's sounds perfect."

The two of them went over to Jane and Jeremy's barely started trench further up the path. Thankfully, a small blue cushion had been provided for her to kneel on.

"I really do hope I don't find anything important."

Jane kneeled beside her and handed her a trowel.

"Aunt Kate, it doesn't matter who makes a find. It's a team effort."

"Yes, but I'm not really part of the team. What if I find a priceless treasure?"

"Just dig a little and we'll analyse things as you go."

Kate eased the trowel into the earth and gave it a wiggle. She then lifted out some soil and tipped it onto an existing heap to her right.

"Nothing to report, Jane."

"No... well, why don't I leave you to it for a bit. If you feel your knees going, just give a yell."

"Righto." Kate supposed that five minutes would be about right – certainly enough for her to talk about her exploits later in the White Horse.

As it was, in half that time the edge of the trowel struck something. She wondered if to ask Jane or Jeremy for guidance but rather than alert them to a wandering root, she scraped around the object a little more until she could be sure.

She then alerted Jane and Jeremy.

"Did the Normans wear glasses?"

They hurried over.

"Oh," said Jane. "They look quite modern."

She summoned the professor, who was quick to join them.

Kate meanwhile had a theory.

"Perhaps someone lost a pair of spectacles on the previous dig."

"It's possible," said Perry. "Let's dig a little further, shall we."

Jane and Jeremy were soon in action, carefully removing enough soil until they could be certain.

"I'm assuming it's not Prior Wilfred," said Kate.

"No," said Perry, eyeing the human skull. "This doesn't date back anything like six centuries. This is much more recent. Perhaps twenty years?"

Four

Having had Harry rouse him at the police house, the tall, young, uniformed Constable Drake arrived in brisk fashion at the trench.

"Well, what have we here?" he puffed.

To Kate, his uniform may have signified authority, but his steel grey eyes showed uncertainty.

"It's a good question," she said.

"Lord Mortimer's not going to like it," said Dennis Wells, a well-built gamekeeper in his mid-fifties. Standing between the constable and Jane, he looked far too warm in a gabardine jacket, and surely there was no need for a shotgun.

Kate was standing behind them squinting against the sun. She felt terrible. Of all the things she might have accomplished on a Saturday afternoon, this would have been bottom of any list.

On the opposite side of the trench, Professor Perry Nash was flanked by Harry, Jeremy, Owen and Cecily Cooper, who, like Dennis Wells, had spotted the uniformed constable hurrying towards the ruin.

"Right," said Perry, mopping his brow with a white cambric handkerchief, "you'll notice that this new trench cuts across an earlier one at a right angle. You can see the body is in the earlier trench."

He didn't mention that only bone remained of the deceased, as that was obvious to any casual observer.

"I see," said Constable Drake, galvanising himself. "And who dug this new trench?"

"My students dug out eighteen inches or so, then Mrs Forbes, as our guest, did some excavating with a trowel, just to get a feel for how archaeology proceeds. I wasn't expecting her to find anything."

"It must have been a shock, Mrs Forbes," said the constable.

"It was," said Kate. "I'll be fine though, thank you."

"Right then…" Constable Drake seemed to wrestle with a few options before settling on one. "Is this earlier trench from the 1908 investigation?"

"Almost certainly," said Perry.

"And do we know who dug it?"

"Will Jessup. He was a hired hand back then."

"Right… and back then I suppose you archaeologists had a good poke around in the trench with trowels."

"Yes, constable, something along those lines."

"With no sign of a body, I'd imagine."

"Quite so."

"So, at some point, you finished your activities and had Will Jessup fill the trench in again."

"Ah, no..." said Perry. "We had limited funds. While digging is hard work, filling in is relatively easy."

"So, one of the team would have filled it in. Yourself, perhaps?"

"I did fill a couple in. Only... well, it's a long time ago, but I think it was on the other side of the field."

"Alright, so who filled this one in?"

"Sorry, I can't remember."

The constable peered back towards Mortimer Hall.

"Ah... his lordship."

All turned in that direction, where the elderly but determined Lord Mortimer, aided by a walking stick, was on the path some fifty yards away, headed in their direction.

"Do you know his lordship?" Kate asked Jane.

"No, only his granddaughter, Ursula from school. I did meet Lord Mortimer when we first arrived, but just to say hello and explain our intentions."

The constable turned to Perry again.

"Professor Nash? Is it right, you're looking for a body?"

"The last resting place of Prior Wilfred, yes, but that's not our main purpose. It's possible he'll never be found."

Constable Drake looked around the site.

"Legend has it there are loads of bodies buried here."

"Yes, but the only ones we can be sure of are those within the priory church footprint. That was the case at the Lewes Priory ruin when the railway was built over the apse. They found the remains of the Earl of Surrey and his wife."

"Really?"

Perry Nash checked on Lord Mortimer, who was still twenty yards off. It was apparent now that he was wearing a chocolate brown three-piece tweed suit that was far too heavy for the warm weather.

"We could find the de Vere family quite easily," Perry continued, "but Prior Wilfred and others were reburied outside to make room for later de Vere generations."

"What does his lordship think of all this digging?"

"Well… he certainly has no interest in digging up the remains of a wealthy family who paid cash for a favourable spot. Those are his words, by the way."

Constable Drake nodded.

"But he was happy to give permission to dig in 1908?"

"Yes, he was keen then and he's still keen today. His son, Teddy, less so."

"What's all this about a body?" a puffing Lord Mortimer demanded as he joined them.

"We know very little at this stage, your lordship," said Constable Drake. "It would appear to be in a trench dug in 1908."

"Incredible! How did it get there?"

"Er, first things first – we need to ascertain a few details from what's in front of us."

"My dear boy, it's clearly a murder victim. Unless you're suggesting this poor soul fell into a trench and somebody inadvertently covered them with soil."

"Murder's a likely theory, your lordship, but I've been trained to take things one step at a time. Do you have any idea who it might be?"

"No, I don't."

Kate felt a pang for the old boy. A tinge of worry was etched into the features below those bushy white eyebrows, while he leaned a little too heavily on his silver-tipped ebony cane.

"I've got a fold-up seat, Lord Mortimer," said Perry Nash. "If you'd like it...?"

"No, no, I'm fine, thank you."

Just then, a thin woman, possibly in her fifties, called out as she hurried at top speed towards them from the direction of the hall. Indeed, the billowing sleeves of her pink crepe de chine dress suggested that flight might be a possibility.

"My husband's on his way... I had to disturb him at his club... in Mayfair."

"Lavinia Mortimer," Jane informed Kate.

All waited for her to join them, which she did in a breathless state.

"To say Teddy was shocked would be an understatement."

"I can imagine," said the constable. "Any idea who we might have here?"

Lavinia looked briefly at the remains. "No, sorry."

"Just to remind you, Mrs Mortimer, we're looking at a trench from the 1908 excavations, if that helps?"

"It doesn't."

She caught sight of Jane.

"Lady Jane, hello again."

"Hello again, Mrs Mortimer. I'm sorry it's turned out so dreadfully."

"I'll tell you something, constable," said Perry, "I suspect this unfortunate individual would have been placed here not long after we finished our work. I say that because all this would have grown over quite quickly."

"Yes… I'd say you're right, which is at least one step towards finding out who's behind it."

"Evil spirits," said Cecily Cooper. "That's who's behind it."

Kate's eyebrows shot up.

"Spirits? No, Mrs Cooper. But evil? Yes, undoubtedly."

Five

At the edge of the trench, Constable Drake dropped to his knees for a closer look. It made Kate wince. Were she to drop to her knees in such a fashion, her next stop would be the hospital.

Professor Nash squatted down beside Drake and proffered a well-used trowel.

"Have you done much of this sort of work, constable?"

"No, but I'll be fine."

Drake began scraping. Indeed, all watched him for five or more fruitless minutes, which, to Kate, felt much longer.

But suddenly he stopped.

"An indented crack on the side of the skull…"

"Some kind of heavy implement, most likely," said Lord Mortimer.

"Indeed." Drake stood up. "As I suspected, it looks like murder."

"This is terrible," cried a worried Lavinia. "It's my granddaughter's christening next weekend."

Kate sympathised.

"I'm sure it can all be sorted out before then."

"You don't understand, Mrs...?"

"Forbes."

"Forbes... yes... you see, we have family and friends arriving on Friday. They'll be staying at the hall. The view of the priory ruin is a highlight. I wouldn't want them looking in this direction right now though."

"I'd better telephone the Chief Constable," said Drake.

"You can use the one at the hall," said Lord Mortimer.

"If it's any help," said Jane, "Aunt Kate and I know someone at Scotland Yard who might be interested."

"It's the weekend," Kate pointed out.

"I'm sure he won't mind being contacted at home," said Jane. "Well, perhaps just a little."

Constable Drake turned to Nash's students.

"Could you get some sheets to cover the body. And if you could stand guard, that would be marvellous. And can I ask everyone else to go home. This is now officially a police matter."

Drake then ran off – leaving Cecily Cooper and Dennis Wells looking somewhat put out as they too departed.

"Inspector Ridley then," said Jane.

"Yes, but let's not rush," said Kate. "We want to give Constable Drake time to explain things to the Chief

Constable. You never know, Scotland Yard may be alerted without our involvement."

Kate and Jane therefore paused before heading to the hall at a sedate pace.

"Jane, explain the Mortimers to me. Is Teddy the heir?"

"No, he's the youngest of Lord Mortimer's three sons. The other two left the hall years ago. I'm not one for gossip, but there are stories of Teddy marrying Lavinia for her money and her marrying him for his status."

"That's a terrible thing to hear… and yet something I've heard all too often down the years. I'm sure they love each other very much."

"Hmm."

"And you were at school with their daughter."

"Ursula, yes. We were at Roedean together. She has a brother, Roger. He's abroad, I think."

"Does Ursula live at the hall?"

"No, she lives in London with her husband, the Honourable Colin Amhurst Camley. She's just down for the week leading up to little Rosie's christening next Sunday."

"Rosie… that's a lovely name."

"Helen Rose Juliette Camley – Rosie for short. Apparently, Lavinia wanted a private christening on Friday, but Ursula stood her ground. She wants as many parishioners there as possible."

"Good for Ursula then."

"She told me the vicar prefers it too."

Just ahead, Lord Mortimer and his daughter-in-law Lavinia came to a halt. Perhaps to wait for Kate and Jane to catch up, or perhaps to allow Lord Mortimer a moment to catch his breath. Either way, all four then proceeded together.

"Just think," said Lord Mortimer, "we're walking the original medieval path between the priory church and the old gatehouse."

"Between the ruin and our lovely gates, you mean?" said Lavinia. She turned to Kate and Jane. "As I understand it, the first Lord Mortimer pulled the old gatehouse down in 1802 because it spoiled the view of the ruin from the hall."

Jane smiled patiently.

As for Kate – she stared at Mortimer Hall with its cream stucco front blazing in the sunlight. It almost dazzled her enough to divert attention from its neat sash windows arranged either side of a portico entrance. It was certainly big. A dozen bedrooms, perhaps?

The four of them soon reached the wide-open iron gates hung on decorative stone pillars. Beyond lay a hundred-yard drive through a wide green space interspersed with oak, ash and beech. There was another sight too – that of Constable Drake hurrying towards them.

"Mrs Forbes, Lady Jane? The Chief Constable says if you could get someone from Scotland Yard down here today, he'd be most grateful."

Kate nodded.

"Inspector Ridley it is then. Hopefully, he's sitting at home bored witless waiting for exactly the sort of call I'm about to make."

Six

Kate returned to the site to find Inspector Ridley with Constable Drake, Professor Nash, Jane and the other students peering down at the unidentified skeletal remains. It had been a long wait for his arrival, which she spent resting in her room at the White Horse Inn.

Ridley's regular dark blue suit and polished black brogues said he was ready for business. Below his hat, a frown on his brow suggested it was a grudging form of readiness.

"Inspector, hello! I hope we haven't spoiled your weekend. Were you tending your roses?"

"Mrs Forbes, I haven't come all this way to discuss gardening. We'll have to unearth the body a bit more – I'll need a specialist."

"You have a team of archaeologists," Jane pointed out, "led by Professor Peregrine Nash of Oxford University."

"Yes, well, seeing as it's a Saturday, that might have to do. Professor, if you wouldn't mind? Let's see what's what without making a mess of it."

"Yes, inspector. That's my usual method."

Just then, Jeremy piped up. "It's a shame you didn't bring your metal detector, Harry."

"What's that?" Ridley asked.

"Oh, nothing much," said Harry. "During the War, they started using battery powered metal detectors to find shallow land mines. I've got one at home, but the professor didn't want it here."

"We discussed that," said Perry. "Metal detectors are not up to the job of locating artefacts buried deep. Mind you, the technology is improving all the time. Who knows, we may one day have armies of amateur treasure hunters digging up half of England."

While Perry began his work, Ridley's attention returned to Kate.

"By the way, Mrs Forbes, good day to you. Now, you found the body. Were you looking in this spot specifically?"

"Yes, although…"

"It was my suggestion," said Jane. "It's an area we're interested in. If you look at the strata, you'll see we've dug at right angles across the 1908 trench."

"Yes, I see. So, who was on the earlier dig?"

"I've made a list," said Constable Drake retrieving his notebook from his breast pocket. "Let me see… we have the Reverend Humphrey Pickton. He's the vicar at St Peter's and he was in charge of the dig. Then we have his informal assistant at the time, Aubrey Enright, who doesn't much like the Mortimers. Then Peregrine Nash... that's before he became a professor. Robert Stone and Francis Best, two students from Oxford. Horace and Victor Enright, who no longer live in Penford. And Ronald Lambert, a local man who died in the War. We also have Will Jessup, who runs the White Horse Inn. Back then, he was a labourer who dug the trenches. I've also got some names who weren't on the dig but were around at the time."

"Go on..."

"Betty Bagnall, who worked at the White Horse at the time and who brought sandwiches and refreshments to the diggers. Lord Mortimer, the landowner. Teddy Mortimer, his son. Then there's Teddy's wife, Lavinia... Dennis Wells, the Mortimers' gamekeeper... and finally, Jim Archer, a grocery delivery boy. He used to come up here to see what was going on."

"When you say delivery boy, how old?"

"He would have been eighteen or so at the time, sir."

"Right..." Ridley puffed out his cheeks. "So that's half the district twenty years ago. Did anyone go missing around that time? Or since?"

"No," said Constable Drake. "It's a bit of a mystery."

"What about you, professor. You were here in 1908."

"Yes, I was what you might call a mature student. I'd studied history for many years, but I was new to archaeology."

"And you haven't been back until now?"

"Actually, I came back to dig about eighteen months ago, but Lord Mortimer was taken ill and Teddy Mortimer cancelled it. He said he didn't want his father overexerting himself popping up here and what-have-you. I was busy after that but managed to see his lordship a few months ago. He agreed to me coming back and… well, here we are."

"And did Teddy Mortimer approve?"

"Of the re-arranged dig?"

"Yes, did Teddy Mortimer give you his blessing?"

"No, he and his wife were dead against it."

"Were they, indeed?"

Over the next thirty minutes, as the earth around the body was carefully removed, certain details were revealed. At this point, Inspector Ridley saw fit to recap.

"Definitely a woman's remains… a thin gold chain with a Pisces astrological sign around the neck… a brooch timepiece… most of the clothing disintegrated… would you say the body's been here twenty years?"

Professor Nash nodded.

"It's not within my usual range, but yes. It's not recent, that's for sure. This is interesting though…" He pointed his trowel at an almost rectangular outline beside the body.

"The damp conditions have done a lot of damage, but it looks like the remains of a large carpet bag."

"Yes, I see…"

"If you look, there's a rotted through purse inside it – in the corner there. In the purse, you'll notice the perished remains of several banknotes. There's also a shilling, a sixpence, and a few pennies."

"Yes, I see."

"Well, here's an oddity. If you look in the opposite corner of the carpet bag, there's another coin."

"Why's that odd?"

"It's gold."

"Gold?"

The professor loosened it and lifted it from the soil.

"It's a Celtic stater."

"A what?"

"The Celts copied Greek coins," Perry Nash explained. "Or as we call them, staters."

"Right, so it's a Celtic copy of a Greek coin," said Ridley.

"Precisely. On this side, it's… well, it's a bad copy, but it's the head of Philip the Second of Macedonia."

"Is it?"

Kate squinted. It looked more like abstract lines and blobs.

"Actually, this is more likely a copy of a copy," Perry continued. "Whereas the original would have had a clear face and a decorative laurel leaf headdress, whoever struck this version was working a little in the dark."

"Yes, I can see it now," said Ridley. "Sort of."

"If we turn it over," said Perry, demonstrating, "it's hard to say what the original design was. Something floral, perhaps."

"Yes, but it's definitely gold?"

"Yes, gold with a little silver and copper added. It's quite a valuable item."

"Interesting," said Ridley.

They watched for a moment as Jane began to make a pencil drawing of the coin's design in a large notebook.

"Strange to have one of these loose in her bag," she noted as she drew.

"That's what I was thinking," said Ridley.

When she'd finished, she handed the coin to the inspector, who wrapped it in a cloth provided by Harry.

"Right," he said, placing the piece of evidence in his pocket, "I'd like everyone here to keep quiet about the gold stater until I've concluded my inquiries. The last thing I need right now is an army of gold diggers turning up."

Just then, a man, possibly in his fifties, came hurrying across the grassy expanse.

"Who's this?" Ridley asked Drake.

"Lord Mortimer's son. Theodore Mortimer – Teddy to all."

"We'll keep the coin from him too. I don't want the site disturbed by anyone – whoever they are."

Seven

Kate and Jane came to the end of a dry track that deposited them onto Priory Street just before a row of three red brick houses. They stopped outside the first of them.

"Here we are," said Kate, noting the sign in the window: 'Police Station'.

The house seemed too small for the job, but she supposed it met Penford's requirements.

There was no need to knock as Inspector Ridley was at the window and, in a flash, at the door.

"Ladies, I've just got here myself. Come in and Constable Drake will take your statements in a moment."

"Thank you, inspector," said Kate, entering the short hallway. "What a lovely house. Both police station and home."

"I do my best," came a voice from the back. It was followed by the appearance of an apron-wearing woman in her fifties with kindly eyes and a ready smile.

"I do admire you," said Kate. "I have enough trouble keeping my own home tidy, but to have it as a police house."

"Mrs Forbes," Ridley urged, "let's get that statement written up, shall we?"

But Mrs Drake wasn't finished.

"My husband, God rest his soul, was a labourer, Mrs Forbes. I can tell you his passing left me with more than a few worries. But then it all came right with Francis here becoming a constable. The police give me a small allowance, and now we have a telephone too."

"It sounds perfect."

"Oh no, it won't be perfect till Frank ties the knot with his Maisie. Two years they've been engaged."

"Mum…" sighed the constable.

Kate smiled. "Mrs Drake, you and your family are a credit to Penford."

"Thank you, Mrs Forbes. It's nice to be appreciated. You must have some tea and cake."

Ridley seemed tetchy.

"Mrs Drake, these ladies are here to make a statement."

"Inspector Ridley, this is my house."

"Yes, I fully appreciate that…"

"They can make their statements once we've had our tea. Now, I made some rock cakes this morning."

"My favourite," said Jane.

"Then we'll have them with a little butter and strawberry jam, my dear."

"Lovely."

Ridley puffed out his cheeks. Apparently, on these premises, Mrs Drake outranked anyone from Scotland Yard.

A few moments later, while Kate and Jane took their seats around a table in the back room, Mrs Drake went off to the kitchen to make the tea. Ridley and the constable reluctantly joined them.

"What a lovely room," said Kate. "I can see your mother is very proud of you, constable." She was indicating the mantelpiece over the tiled fire surround. "Is that a scout badge?"

Constable Drake went across to retrieve it – a thick cotton fleur-de-lys design mounted on a card.

"It's actually me who kept it. I was Penford's first boy scout. The vicar was scout master. This was... well, 1908."

"I'm sure it was a happy time," said Kate.

"It was. Scouting changed the course of my life. I don't think I'd have become a policeman if it weren't for the scouts."

"Wonderful," said Jane. "A scout's honour is everything. He can be trusted. He's loyal and will do his duty. A friend to all."

Drake smiled. "That's right, Lady Jane."

"I was in the Girl Guides."

"Oh well, then you know everything I know about duty and doing good turns."

Ridley frowned.

"I'm sure this is all very commendable, but I've come down from London to solve a murder – and that's more likely to happen if witnesses furnish me with prompt statements."

"Statements *and theories?*" Kate wondered. "I'm assuming you're thinking the body was planted at the priory site in 1908, most likely just after the team left."

"Within days or weeks," said Jane. "Months possibly – but even a year later it would have grown over."

Kate nodded. "Someone made use of a freshly dug trench for a quick job, inspector."

"Mrs Forbes, for what it's worth, may I remind you that you're not investigating this case."

"There's no need for a reminder, inspector. Jane and I will keep well out of it. Won't we, Jane."

"Yes, although I'm curious about the gold stater. It doesn't make sense."

"You leave that to me, Lady Jane. Although, I have to agree it's an oddity. That said, sometimes a case is too old for us to make any meaningful progress. This might be one of them. Now tell me something – how does it work if you find anything of value?"

"That's easy. Lord Mortimer's the landowner – he owns anything we find. There's an agreement in place though. His lordship would make a contribution to a library in Oxford. I think in 1908, it was a contribution to the church fabric fund. Of course, a small religious item might find its way to the parish church."

A knock at the front door interrupted them.

Constable Drake went off to investigate immediately, while those at the table were soon listening in on raised voices.

"Hello, Jim? Have you come to make a statement."

"What? No. I just heard they found Rebecca Shaw."

"That's right. Seeing as you were around when she… disappeared, I'd like a statement."

"I don't know anything apart from the lies you're likely to hear."

"What lies?"

"I know it's none of my business, but whatever you hear from Lavinia Mortimer about being all friendly with Rebecca, it's not true. She never liked her. Not a bit."

"Jim, whenever anything happens in Penford, there's usually enough gossip to launch a fleet of hot air balloons."

"I swear it, Frank. It's what I saw a couple of times – a look of hate. No doubt about it."

"Right… and did you witness any exchanges between them?"

"Exchanges of what?"

"Words."

"Oh… not actual words, no. But if looks could kill…"

"Alright, Jim, I'll definitely want a signed statement."

"Not now, I'm busy. You just make sure Scotland Yard's bloke knows. If anyone had a reason to do away with Rebecca, it would be someone who hated her."

"Alright, I'll tell the inspector right away. But I'll be after you later for that statement. No excuses."

Constable Drake returned to the back room.

"Jim Archer…"

"Yes, we heard," said Ridley.

"That was interesting about Lavinia Mortimer," said Kate.

"Assuming it's true," Ridley reminded her.

"Oh, absolutely, inspector."

As Mrs Drake came in with the tea, Kate smiled. But her thoughts remained with Jim Archer. Was he an honourable man coming forward with information? Or was he a troublemaker with an agenda?

Eight

Early on Saturday evening in the White Horse Inn, Kate and Jane were coming down the stairs into the first-class lounge. While the September sun had crowned the day, the evening was a little chillier and they were happy to remain inside, where a fire glowed and electric lamps had been lit despite there still being some daylight left.

At the bar stood a man in his late thirties in a slightly-too-big black checked jacket that didn't match his navy-blue trousers. He was with cigarette-smoking Aubrey Enright and the elderly Sidney Allen, who was smoking a stinky pipe.

"No, no, Jim, you've got it all wrong," Aubrey was telling the younger man, leading Kate to wonder if this might be Jim Archer.

Seated a good distance from them, over by one of the front windows, cigar-smoking Teddy Mortimer was in conversation with Dennis Wells, his gamekeeper.

All five men were drinking the same dark ale, as were three others in another corner.

If the Enrights and Mortimers didn't get on, then perhaps the situation required tact.

"Shall we sit over there," Kate suggested to her niece, indicating a table on the other side of the room, away from all parties.

"Can I get you a drink, ladies?" called Will Jessup from behind the bar.

"Ah, thank you," said Kate. "A small dry sherry for me. Jane?"

"A gin and tonic, please."

"Coming right up."

They took their seats at the freshly polished table.

"Under normal circumstances, this would be a lovely place to spend a day or two," said Jane.

"Absolutely," said Kate. "I wonder if Aubrey Enright and Teddy Mortimer ever enjoy a convivial pint of ale together."

Not wishing to look in the direction of either, she peered through the arch that led to the public lounge, where a few agricultural workers were noisily enjoying themselves.

Just then, a smiling woman in her sixties emerged from the staff door behind the bar and came over to their table.

"Good evening, I'm Betty. Now, I've got a lovely shepherd's pie in the oven, if that pleases. Or I could grill you some lamb chops?"

Kate wasn't sure.

"Jane?"

"Shepherd's pie for me, please, Betty. It's been a long day."

"Yes, me too then," said Kate. "But a small portion or I won't be able to move from this chair."

"I know what you mean," said Betty.

"Do the Mortimers and Enrights ever take a day off from disliking each other?" asked Kate in a low voice.

Betty glanced one way then the other.

"Things haven't been too bad lately. I think this poor soul you found... well, it's gone right around the village. I mean people have started to wonder about other people."

"You mean Teddy Mortimer and Aubrey Enright don't trust each other," Jane surmised.

"Yes, well... I'm Betty Bagnall, a widow, but I was born an Enright. Not that I let it get in the way of things. Now, I'll see about your shepherd's pie. Be half an hour or so."

They watched her go before Jane spoke again.

"This is usually a great part of the day for archaeologists. A long stint outside, digging, sifting, analysing, discussing findings and prospects..."

"Sitting in the pub afterwards, you mean."

"Yes, but not today. All I can think of is that poor woman."

"Me too," said Kate. "What a terrible end. And then to be lost to the world for twenty years."

"At least she'll have a decent burial now."

"Yes, well... someone in Penford knows something about it, Jane. Someone here knows the truth."

Jane glanced across to Aubrey Enright's group, and then to Teddy Mortimer and his gamekeeper.

Kate raised an eyebrow. "I wasn't suggesting anyone in this pub."

Her niece nodded, which seemed to neither rule these drinkers in nor out.

Meanwhile, Aubrey Enright drained his tankard and placed it on the counter. With that, he turned to Kate and Jane.

"What a business!" he pronounced. "You ladies must still be in shock."

Kate appreciated his concern.

"We are, to a degree. Unfortunately, it's not our first experience of discovering a body, which I suppose has aided our recovery. It's not something to be proud of, but there we have it. Jane and I are a little shaken, but perfectly fine."

Aubrey Enright looked puzzled.

"May I ask where you encountered such a thing previously? War work, was it?"

"No, we've... shall we say *assisted* Inspector Ridley before."

"I see... so, what does he think about it then?"

"We're not privy to that. At least not yet."

Aubrey pressed the stub of his cigarette into a metal ashtray on the counter.

"I wonder how many other bodies are buried up there," he mused.

Kate suspected this comment was more for Teddy Mortimer than herself or her niece.

"None from recent times, I'm sure," Teddy duly responded. "It's the Mortimer estate, not a battlefield. That said, I'm as concerned as anyone to get some answers."

Jim Archer nodded. "I'm sure we're all keen to see justice done, Mr Mortimer. If there's anything I can do to help, I'll do it."

Teddy smiled. "I'm glad to hear it, Jim, but I think we'll leave it to the police. This Ridley chap seems to know what's what."

Kate recognised Jim's voice – which now confirmed him as Jim Archer who called at the police house. What was he up to though? Hadn't he told Constable Drake that Teddy's wife should be considered a suspect?

Just then, the landing above them creaked and footsteps hit the wooden stairs. A moment later, Professor Peregrine Nash was nodding to the company and joining Kate and Jane at their table.

"Anything for you, professor?" Will asked.

"A glass of ale, please, landlord."

"Coming right up."

While Jim Archer and Teddy Mortimer continued their concerned exchange, the ladies' attention was taken by Perry.

"Sorry for the delay, ladies. I fell asleep. To be truthful, I didn't sleep much last night. I think I ate too much of the shepherd's pie. Best avoided, I think. What are you ladies having for dinner, by the way?"

About ten minutes later, Teddy Mortimer got up from his table, leaving his gamekeeper seated.

"I'll see you in the morning, Wells."

"Righto, guvnor."

Teddy looked across to those at the bar, and to Kate's table.

"Have a good evening, all."

He left to farewells from Kate, Jane, the professor, Sid, Jim and Will.

Aubrey Enright grunted somewhat and, no sooner the door had closed, turned to Will.

"I expect you've heard the rumours?"

"I never listen to rumours, Mr Enright. You know that."

"Well, I've been hearing about Teddy Mortimer and this woman having had an affair. And what's more, I heard he got rid of her."

"That's a terrible thing to say."

"They've got a long history of ill-treating people. When I was a boy, we had a saying – that the Mortimers think they can treat you as badly as they like as long as they put a few pennies in your hand."

"None of that's evidence," said Jim. "Evidence has to be facts, something you've seen with your own eyes."

Aubrey sneered.

"It's the Mortimers we're talking about. The Mortimers, boy. Anyway, it came from a reliable source. That's all you need to know. The facts of the matter put Teddy Mortimer in a bad light. It won't be long before Scotland Yard's man works it out."

Kate suspected that Aubrey Enright would happily give things a shove in that direction with a word in the inspector's ear. Fortunately, Ridley wasn't one to be swayed by gossip. She also wondered about Jim Archer. His words at the police house – and now his dislike of idle gossip.

"Mr Enright?" asked Jane.

"Yes?"

"We've assisted the inspector in the past. He'll be interested to know that you dislike the Mortimers. He'll take it into account should you speak to him."

Aubrey looked annoyed.

Meanwhile, Dennis Wells stood up.

"The inspector might also be interested to know it was Aubrey Enright who filled in that trench where the body was found."

Aubrey's annoyance turned into outright shock.

"I don't recall that...?"

"It was out of my mind for a long time, Mr Enright," said Dennis, "but it came back to me. You were on that side of the priory field late in the day, filling in the trench farthest up on that side. I remember hoping you might fall in."

With that, Dennis Wells turned and left.

Nine

Kate rode out the moment of awkwardness by following a puff of smoke from Sid Allen's pipe all the way up to the ceiling.

"Coaching inns are fascinating," said Perry Nash, no doubt in an attempt to recapture a degree of conviviality. "Did you know they were often spaced seven miles apart?"

Kate, for one, did not.

"Seven miles? Ah, the horses, I expect."

"Yes," said Perry. "Before the railways, at every seven-mile stage, the *stage*-coach would stop at a coaching inn for a change of horses."

"Such as the White Horse," Kate suggested.

"Yes, such as this fine establishment. In larger towns, there would be a number of them fighting for custom."

"Upton," said Will Jessup, his landlord's ears tuned to the only conversation in the room. "That's where the London railway came through."

"It's quite handy," said Jim Archer.

"If you live in Upton," said Sid Allen.

"I'm just saying it's handy," Jim protested.

"What are you on about?" said Aubrey. "I doubt you've been on a train since the War ended."

"Yeah, well, I had enough of trains back then."

"A lot of men had enough of trains back then," said Sid.

Kate sympathised. During the War, countless trains took countless men to Folkestone Harbour to board the boat to France. Many never returned.

"I'm not complaining," said Jim. "I spent the War distributing food supplies to hundreds of army kitchens. I saw the casualties being loaded on the trains back to England though."

An awkward silence descended.

"I'm sure the White Horse has a fair future," said Perry, once again gamely attempting to lighten the mood. "Judging by the number of motor vehicles on the road these days, I expect Penford's passing trade to increase over the coming years."

"Wise words," said Aubrey Enright. "Penford will regain its place over Upton. Before the 1850s we were twice the size of them."

"And now Upton's twice the size of us," said Jim. "It's a proper town now, whereas…"

"Whereas we're back on track," said Aubrey.

"Oh!" laughed Sid. "Back on track. Track, see... like the railways... very funny..."

Aubrey studiously ignored him.

"Penford will rise again," he said with pride. "I, myself, plan on opening a petrol station with a motor spares and repair business. I've already invested £80 in buying the land."

"That's very enterprising," said Perry. "Your customers could take refreshment here in the White Horse while they wait for repairs to be carried out."

Landlord Will Jessup laughed.

"Yeah, keep 'em waiting a good few days, Mr Enright. As the professor says, that would be very enterprising."

Kate didn't like such underhand talk.

"Perhaps you could advertise in London," she suggested to Will. "Your inn is a good place to break a road journey to the coast. People need to know you're here."

"Yes, that's an idea, I suppose," said Will, his face showing that this hadn't previously occurred to him. "I usually advertise in Upton and the local area, but London..."

"You could describe the White Horse as steeped in history," Perry suggested. "That should get them interested."

"Steeped in history... now *there's* a thought."

Aubrey put his drink down.

"If it's advertising expertise you need, I can help you."

"Oh?"

"Show me that paper," he said, pointing to a folded edition of the local newspaper on the shelf behind the bar.

Will attempted to hand it to Aubrey but the latter's finger simply drew the landlord's attention to something at the foot of the front page.

"Read that."

Will squinted at the print.

"Let me see… 'People need to live and the living need to eat and drink. For life's necessities, visit Enright's Modern Grocery Stores. The proprietor and his family are waiting to supply you with the best at a fair price.'"

"Penford is growing," said Aubrey. "The National Omnibus Transport Company are planning a bus route through Penford starting next year. There are also plans for a new bakery to save us from relying on deliveries from Upton."

"Fascinating," said Kate. "It looks like the village has a bright future."

"Yeah, things have picked up since the War," said Will.

"They certainly have for you, Mr Jessup. As a young man, you were a labourer."

"That's right, although at the same time I was learning the ropes here helping Jack Ramsey with serving customers, taking in deliveries and what-have-you. What you won't know is that a strand of the Jessup family did very well in haulage up in the Midlands. When Jack retired, a second cousin of mine was able to help me take over."

"I remember Old Jack's time," said Sid. "Terrible, it was. Damp and dusty. Will's done a good job. Mind you, he's had to work hard."

Kate wondered if Sid was trying to earn himself a free drink.

"Yes, a good hard worker," Aubrey agreed. "You'll find plenty of us in Penford. You'll also find lazy good-for-nothings thinking they're better than us. They're not though, that's a fact. Take those Mortimers. Are their titles edible? Because I'll tell you this, should the ordinary folk walk away, would any single Mortimer know how to bring about a harvest of any kind?"

Kate respected his right to an opinion, but that didn't mean she had to like him.

"I heard that a couple of young Enrights were on the 1908 dig," she said in an attempt to take the wind out of his sails.

Aubrey visibly bristled.

"Horace and Victor Enright are respectable men! One has a furniture shop in Brighton, the other works for a brewery in London. What are you insinuating?"

Just then, Inspector Ridley came in through the front door looking very much like a man who wasn't enjoying his weekend.

"Any luck?" Will Jessup asked, most likely pleased for the interruption.

"It's early stages," said Ridley. "I'll be speaking to everyone who was around during the 1908 dig, regardless of their role."

Jim Archer frowned.

"Speaking to everyone? You mean tonight?"

"No, tomorrow morning."

"Best not have hangovers then, boys," said Sid. He followed this jocular observation with an extended wheezy cough.

Ridley meanwhile huffed and made his way out to the back, calling as he did so.

"I'll be in the incident room if anyone has any information they haven't put in their statement to Constable Drake."

"What incident room?" questioned Jim.

Will Jessup got in first.

"The inspector's booked a room to sleep in, but he's also taken the back room to be an incident room. He reckons the police house is too small."

Jim called after Ridley.

"Hey! We've got a darts match in there later – Penford West against Penford East!"

Ridley stopped and turned. He clearly considered the protest for a couple of seconds before delivering a final decision on the matter.

"Darts is cancelled."

"Cancelled?" gasped Jim.

Aubrey Enright attempted to placate him.

"It's only for a few days. Once they've charged the Mortimers with murder, everything will get back to normal."

Kate was appalled, but a rumbling on the stairs cut off any retort. Harry, Jeremy and Owen were coming down to join them.

Indeed, within half an hour another dozen customers had come into the first-class lounge, while the songs in the public lounge became noisy enough to disturb Inspector Ridley, who emerged from his incident room clutching his papers and made for the stairs.

"Darts is back on," he informed those at the bar, which resulted in a resounding cheer.

Kate felt sorry for him. But there were compensations. With the pub now much busier, she could no longer see or hear Aubrey Enright.

It would be a pleasant evening after all, she felt. Pleasant, but not perfect – thanks to a question that was surely now in most people's minds.

Who killed Rebecca Shaw?

Ten

On a sunny Sunday morning, Kate and Jane were strolling up to St Peter's, the parish church for Penford, Upton, and the nearby hamlets. It was wonderful to be able to dress for summer, even though they were well into September. Hence, Kate had opted for a thin blue cardigan over a cream floral day dress, while Jane wore a pale-yellow summer jacket over a white blouse.

Approaching the church, Kate admired its cemented rock rubble walls, tiled roof, and shingle spire. But it was the stone window and door surrounds that spoke most profoundly of the dissolved priory church.

With the weather being so fair, quite a few parishioners had delayed their entry and gathered into twos and threes on the grassy patch between the lychgate and the main door. Jane nudged her aunt as they joined them.

"We're five minutes early. Shall we see if we can pick up any interesting gossip?"

Kate glanced at the Mortimers.

Lavinia looked sunny in a wide-brimmed yellow hat, a cream cardigan over a mauve dress with pearls and a stylish silver clutch bag. Ursula looked no less radiant in a pink pastel sleeveless dress with matching shoes. They were chatting with the vicar about next week's baptism. Teddy, meanwhile, was smoking a cigar and listening to Lord Mortimer's views on motor cars. No one would have ever guessed a dead body had been unearthed on their land.

"Teddy does smoke a nice cigar, Jane."

"Cuban, most likely. There are a few importers in London."

Kate noticed how some of the fresh arrivals glanced in Teddy's direction. She could almost hear the disapproving mutterings. No matter the individual, adverse gossip would always have a corrosive effect.

Perhaps pretending to be oblivious to it all, Teddy threw the cigar down and crushed it underfoot before going inside. Lord Mortimer followed. As did Lavinia.

Kate sympathised.

"Inspector Ridley's going to have a job establishing the facts, Jane. Penford's already made up its mind."

"Mrs Forbes? Jane?"

Kate and Jane's attention turned to Ursula Camley. She clearly had a bee in her bonnet.

"What a beautiful morning," said Kate, prior to the usual greetings taking place.

"I wish you'd taken up my invitation, Jane," said Ursula.

"It was very thoughtful, Ursula, but it's research-based fieldwork and I need to be with my colleagues… and my aunt too. She's part of the team."

"It's alright," said Ursula. "I understand. There's something else I'd like to discuss though. I expect you've heard the rumours about my father."

"We take no notice of gossip," said Kate.

"Very wise, Mrs Forbes, but I'm beginning to think the village has decided the matter of who killed Rebecca Shaw."

"It'll pass," said Jane. "Like any storm."

"Yes, but it's Rosie's christening next Sunday and all this mudslinging is casting a cloud over it, if you'll excuse the mixed metaphors. You mentioned a storm. It hasn't begun yet, but it might be thundering down come Friday when my husband returns from business in London with half his family in tow."

Kate felt a pang of sympathy.

"Inspector Ridley will act as quickly as he can. I'll tell you now though, he won't be swayed by a mob. Hard facts and a thorough investigation – that's how he reaches his conclusions. I'm sure your father has nothing to fear."

"Rebecca was our governess for almost a year," said Ursula. "My brother and me were very fond of her."

"Yes, of course…"

"We were disappointed when she left without saying goodbye. Shocked, in fact. Our parents told us she was in a hurry to catch a train."

"So, you saw her one final time before bed?" asked Jane.

"Yes."

"And the next morning she was gone?"

"Yes, before we got up. I think we were at breakfast wondering where she was when Mother told us."

"As you say – a shock."

To Kate it suggested a last-minute decision, otherwise Rebecca would have said goodbye the previous evening. As for the reasons behind it though…

"I don't think I've heard about your brother?" she said.

"Roger's in India with the Army. I'm due to write to him next weekend. I'd like to report a happy family event."

"Yes, of course."

Ursula hesitated for a moment.

"Could you both… well… could you look into it?"

Kate was a little taken aback.

"I'm not sure I follow."

"The speculation will do my father untold damage, regardless of the inspector's efforts. I was wondering… well, hoping really, if you and Jane might help clear up what happened."

Kate considered it.

"Jane and I believe in supporting justice, but this would very much appear to be a police matter."

"Aunt Kate's right," said Jane.

"Absolutely," said Ursula, nodding in agreement, "but I've heard via the noble grapevine that you're a capable duo. Are you sure you couldn't look into it?"

"Ursula!" It was Lavinia Mortimer at the church door.

"I have to go," said Ursula.

"Hello there!" declared the vicar, coming up behind them. "New faces are always welcome at St Peter's."

"Ah vicar, thank you. I'm Mrs Kate Forbes from Sandham-on-Sea and this is my niece, Lady Jane Scott from London. You may have seen Jane around – she's part of the archaeological team."

"Yes, of course. Humphrey Pickton, vicar of St Peter's, at your service. Did I hear mention of a judgemental congregation?"

"Oh… it's simply that justice requires clear heads, not minds that are already made up."

"Yes, the body at the priory does appear to have sparked a great deal of speculation. I sometimes wonder if gossip is a form of entertainment for some. It's the most unreliable way to learn anything and yet it remains an unstoppable force."

"I quite agree, vicar."

"I mean first it's Teddy Mortimer, and now poor Aubrey Enright's name is beginning to rattle along the grapevine due to him being the one who filled in that trench."

All three looked across to Aubrey, who was coming up the church path with his cousin, Betty Bagnall.

Aubrey, though, was suddenly fending off Cecily Cooper who had come hurrying up to him asking, "Is it true?"

"Yes, I filled in the trench," he responded with some agitation, "but I would have noticed a body in it!"

"Poor Aubrey," said the vicar. "he's a proud man."

Kate felt sorry for him.

"Does he have much family?" she wondered.

"There are quite a few Enrights in Penford, although most of them go about their business without drawing attention to themselves."

"...or spending time with Aubrey," Jane noted.

"What about this Ronald Lambert chap who died in the War?" Kate asked.

"An upstanding young man," said the vicar. "His family runs the mill. They're a real asset to the community – employing local men, buying grain from local farmers..."

"The current dig is well under way," said Jane, possibly trying to get them back on track.

"Hmm, indeed," said the vicar. "You know I led the team twenty years ago."

"Did you ever think to try again?" asked Jane.

"Yes, but Lavinia Mortimer blocked it. She thought we made a mess in 1908. She said the site looked like a freshly dug graveyard. Apparently, it gave her sleepless nights. When I suggested another dig the following year, she made such a fuss that Lord Mortimer caved in. I did persist in trying to change his mind, but to no avail."

"Interesting," said Kate.

"Anyhow, I look forward to the professor seeking my opinion should he need to. You will remind him, won't you, Lady Jane?"

"Yes, of course, vicar. I'm sure you'll be consulted."

Kate smiled but doubted that Perry Nash would seek the opinion of a man who had proven himself to be clueless.

"Well, I'd better be getting along," said the vicar with a cheery smile before heading inside.

No sooner he'd disappeared, Professor Nash called out to them. He was coming through the lychgate with Harry, Owen and Jeremy.

"What a lovely morning," he declared. "I've already been over to the site. Not to dig; just to absorb the atmosphere."

"And why not!" Kate enthused.

Greetings were swiftly exchanged followed by Harry, Owen and Jeremy going inside. Kate meanwhile saw to it that the professor lingered a moment longer.

"Perry, you were here twenty years ago – what exactly did you pick up on this feud between the Mortimers and the Enrights?"

"Not much. It wasn't any of my business."

"Of course, but a woman has been murdered, which changes things somewhat. Are you able to disclose any local insight you may have encountered at the time."

"Local insight? You mean gossip?"

Perry drew them aside, away from any potential prying ears.

"Alright, seeing as it's a murder investigation... my first time here, I gathered right away that an inter-family dispute between the Enrights and the Mortimers existed."

"What started it?" asked Kate.

Perry sighed. He clearly preferred historical research to the murky world of motive, means and opportunity.

"It's hardly the Wars of the Roses, Kate..."

"Yes, but?"

Just then, the verger appeared at the church door urging the stragglers to come inside.

As they made their way, Kate nudged Perry's elbow.

"You were saying...?"

"Ah yes... well, as I understand it... back in 1902, Lord Mortimer killed Aubrey Enright's uncle."

Eleven

Kate and Jane were seated on freshly polished pews at the back of the church with Peregrine Nash wedged between them. While the occasion was spiritual, it was somewhat offset by three men in front of them smelling of last night's beer and discussing the bawdy songs they had got through at the Royal Oak.

Fortunately, Kate was able to focus on Perry, who had more to say about Aubrey Enright's uncle.

"According to the story I heard," he said in a suitably low voice, "Lord Mortimer's horse and carriage knocked Aubrey's Uncle Stanley down. The problem is there are two versions. An Enright will say his lordship was drunk. A Mortimer will tell you this Enright chap stepped into the road and spooked the horse. I honestly couldn't tell you which is true."

Kate puffed out her cheeks.

"That's quite a story."

"There's more. As you probably know, the Mortimers own agricultural land. They don't get their hands dirty, of course, but they have a lot of tenant farmers. Going back to the end of the last century, one of the families paying rent was the Enrights. As you're no doubt aware, Aubrey Enright has come a long way since then, but he's acutely aware of his past."

"Interesting," said Kate.

"Now, there's also Dennis Wells. Apparently, he's more than a gamekeeper. Out on the land, he runs things for them. Shooting, fishing, that sort of thing."

"Yes," said Kate, "a loyal Mortimer man, by the look of it."

"He is," said Perry. "Well, the Mortimers still have a number of tenant farmers. They say Dennis Wells makes sure they pay up on time. Apparently, he can be very persuasive. That's according to the Enrights, of course. The Mortimers will tell you he's a lovely chap."

"Yes, I see."

"Then there's Jim Archer. His mother was an Enright – Aubrey's sister, in fact. I think she died a few years back. As for Jim, he runs the grocer's shop with his wife. Jim was eighteen when Rebecca died – and as a young man, he'd be out on his bike doing deliveries. From what I've heard, he had a liking for Rebecca that wasn't reciprocated."

"That's very interesting, Perry."

The professor then indicated Cecily Cooper across the aisle.

"Mrs Cooper was always hanging around back then. She still does to an extent. She's against us disturbing any dead that reside there. Then there's Betty Bagnall sitting with her. Rebecca's arrival at Mortimer Hall meant there was no role for a nanny, a job Betty had held. Obviously, the children were growing up, so it was no surprise, but Betty might have disliked Rebecca."

Any further disclosures were halted by the vicar at the front, hands raised. With sunlight streaming through the stained-glass window behind him, he looked quite the visionary.

"Welcome, welcome!" he declared. "Before this morning's service, I want to say a few words about Rebecca Shaw. As you know, her remains were discovered by the priory ruin. We shall offer a prayer shortly, but before we do, could I caution against idle speculation. It's not at all helpful. If you have any genuine information regarding Rebecca or the 1908 archaeological dig at the priory, please speak to the police."

The vicar then said a prayer for Rebecca before giving his sermon. Unusually though, he began with a brief history of the priory before settling on his main theme – unity.

"Why didn't people fight back to save the monasteries? Hundreds of religious establishments were lost. Thousands of monks, nuns, friars, and canons were thrown onto the streets. And yet the people did nothing. However, what you might not know is that there was widespread discontent among both secular and ecclesiastical rulers in

England. Monasteries were mocked for being lax, worldly, wasteful and superstitious. People questioned why monks were supported by money that could have been better spent on training them to serve as parish priests."

Kate digested this appraisal. She supposed that Henry the Eighth hardly held back from letting the populous know that monks deserved to be punished.

"The dissolution of the monasteries was a cruel, overzealous act," continued the vicar, "and yet it highlighted a genuine issue. From my own extensive research – which is available to Professor Nash and his team – I've learned that 11th and 12th century monastic houses were blessed with revenues from landed estates and parish churches. By Henry the Eight's time, they owned a quarter of the nation's landed wealth. Indeed, had the Abbot of Glastonbury joined forces with the Abbess of Shaftesbury, they would have owned more land than the King!"

Perry nodded appreciatively.

"I have to say the vicar's improved his game. I must have a chat with him."

"Balance!" cried the vicar. "That's the way we choose today. While some are in cloisters still, most are out in the world. Hence myself standing before you in this church and serving you in the parish. This is how the Church and the people can live and worship in partnership."

Three rows ahead of Kate, Aubrey Enright leaned forward towards Teddy Mortimer.

"How can you sit in God's house with murder on your conscience?"

Teddy and Lavinia both turned.

"How dare you!" protested the latter.

The vicar coughed politely.

"As I was saying, our theme this morning is unity."

Twelve

After the service, as people streamed out of St Peter's, Kate left Jane talking to Lord Mortimer, while she tackled Lavinia and Teddy. With Ursula's request in mind, she had already posed a couple of gentle questions about the governess.

Teddy was smiling sadly.

"I liked her very much. She was caring and efficient. She had a pleasant manner about her too. I think everyone liked her."

Kate smiled sadly too.

"I understand the children got on well with her."

"Yes, absolutely. Rebecca taught them to read and to play the piano a little. She also got them outside in the fresh air. I recall her taking Roger and Ursula up to the dig site a few times. She fostered in them a hunger to be curious about the world."

"I think Roger just wanted to join in with the digging," said Lavinia.

Teddy laughed a little before continuing.

"All these years... I was hoping Rebecca might have been happy somewhere."

"Yes, it's tragic," said Kate. "Utterly so. I have to say that others have mentioned your fondness for the poor woman."

Teddy reacted.

"Be careful who you listen to, Mrs Forbes. There are those – even here this morning – who would happily feed you a diet of scandalous lies."

"Yes, we've already heard a thing or two."

"Ours was a proper relationship between employer and employee. Nothing more. Any salacious tittle-tattle about an affair... well... I'll leave you to be the judge."

Lavinia's smile seemed more than simply supportive of her husband. It carried something of a threat.

"I never listen to gossip," said Kate.

"I'm glad to hear it," said Lavinia. "I would hate the lies of the Enright clan to be spread by those who know nothing of their true motives."

"I can assure you that won't happen."

"I despise wagging tongues, Mrs Forbes, but this isn't idle gossip. It's malicious. Rebecca Shaw was a friendly presence under our roof. I was very fond of her."

Kate's thoughts raced back to Jim Archer's view on that – the one he gave to Constable Drake at the police house.

Before more could be said though, Lavinia took her husband's elbow and led him away.

"Gossiping again, Aunt?"

Jane had sidled up unseen, having been partly shielded by Sid Allen..

"You'd make a good spy, Jane. As it was, we were in agreement that gossip's a terrible thing."

"Oh, that's a pity. I've just heard some juicy bits and bobs from his lordship. But as you say, it's beneath us."

"Jane, we seem to have drifted into an investigation of sorts, so anything that might cast light on a potential motive must be considered."

"Well, in terms of gossip, Betty Bagnall is the fountainhead."

"The woman who helps in the White Horse?"

"Yes, Aubrey Enright's cousin."

They peered across at Betty, who had got Teddy Mortimer to one side. She seemed to be putting him in an awkward spot, but it came to an end when Lavinia butted in.

"What about Mr Wells?" Jane wondered, after he had walked past.

"According to facts or gossip?"

"All I know is he's an early riser as he's responsible for everything on the estate."

"I wonder what the inspector makes of him." Kate was eyeing Ridley, who had just invited Dennis Wells to one side.

"There's only one reliable way to find out, Aunt."

They moved a little closer, possibly hoping to blend in with the church architecture.

"I'm not interested in gossip," Ridley was saying, "even though I've been told you're someone who doesn't like taking 'no' for an answer. Right now, I'm more interested in learning how you became the Mortimers' gamekeeper."

"Did the Enrights put you up to this?"

"Just answer the question, Mr Wells."

"It's not a secret. For quite a few years, I worked for Old Tom, the previous gamekeeper. I took over when something happened to him."

"What happened to him?"

"He had an accident. He drowned."

"When was this?"

"Years ago."

"Mr Wells!"

"The summer of 1912."

"And you were on hand to step into the dead man's shoes?"

"That's not how it was."

"Isn't it? Have you killed any poachers?"

"Look, I'm firm in seeing them off, alright? And, for the record, I don't just go after poachers. I rear pheasant and partridge, I make sure the wild grouse thrive, I look after habitats, and I get rid of pests and predators. I'm no murderer, inspector."

"I never said you were. Now tell me, how well did you know Rebecca Shaw?"

"Hardly at all. She was a nice girl with a ready smile. Not just for me, for anyone who worked on the estate. Now, I have to be getting on. If you'll excuse me."

As Dennis Wells departed, Ridley latched onto Kate and Jane.

"Listening in on police business?"

"Certainly not," said Kate. "But I'm sure he makes a good gamekeeper regardless of how he got the job."

"In September 1908, he would have been up early looking for poachers. Rebecca Shaw was up early. I'll leave that thought with you."

They watched him head off in search of other targets.

"What might we construe, Jane? Rebecca Shaw was a wonderful addition to the community, and yet somebody killed her."

"Mrs Forbes?"

Kate's attention turned to Ursula Camley.

"Ah, I expect you're looking for an answer."

"Yes."

Kate smiled.

"Ursula… we've already started."

"Oh, thank goodness."

"Unfortunately, we're already mired in difficulties. For instance, did the killer come from the Mortimer family, or the village, or the archaeological team? And how will we succeed in ruling your father out when he's already one of our main suspects."

"There are no pre-conditions," said Ursula. "It's the truth that matters. I just happen to believe that Father is innocent. I also believe that Inspector Ridley won't have anyone's reputation in mind. I fear he'll pursue justice regardless of the cost."

"That's often the way of things."

"I'd investigate it myself, but I can't imagine the Enrights answering my questions."

"No, neither can I. Now, you were young at the time. Do you recall anything unusual in the days before Rebecca left?"

"No, nothing at all."

"The thing is," said Jane, "the police are already looking into those who were around at the time, but it's the motive they'll become most interested in. If you could help us with that…?"

"I'm not sure I can."

Kate shook her head. "That won't do at all, Ursula. We're already putting ourselves in Inspector Ridley's way. We need to know you're not hiding anything from us, otherwise… what's the point?"

Jane took over. "Inspector Ridley will come up with a motive for the case against your father. You don't really want us to be a step behind the police, do you?"

Ursula looked down at her shoes. "It must be that Father got rid of Rebecca to avoid a scandal. You know, to protect the family's reputation."

"Do you believe it?" said Kate.

Ursula looked up.

"Come back to the hall. I'll persuade Grandfather, Mother and Father to tell you everything they know."

With that, she turned and headed off to the Mortimer car, a large black Bentley, waiting for her in the road.

"That's more like it," said Kate.

Thirteen

Mortimer Hall was just far enough from the church to make Kate wonder if to nip back to the White Horse Inn to get Gertie. Luckily, laziness was overcome, and she and Jane were soon approaching the hall on foot having enjoyed a rewarding amble that took in butterflies, bees, and birdsong.

"Just think," said Kate, "a woman set out from here twenty years ago and disappeared – not just from life but from memory. I find it incredibly sad."

"Me too," said Jane, pausing just short of the gates to the hall's extensive grounds.

"What is it?" said Kate, stopping beside her.

Jane turned to face the ruin, a hundred yards or so away.

"Not only is it private land, it's also visible from a number of directions."

She waved towards a small group by the ruin. Among them, Harry and Owen waved back.

"Not the sort of place you would choose to bury a body then," said Kate.

"No, there's far too much risk of being spotted as a trespasser."

They headed through the gates and up the long gravel drive to the house, where they were met at the front door by Hill the butler.

"Good morning," said Kate. "Mrs Forbes and Lady Jane Scott. We're expected."

Hill showed them into the vestibule while he went to inform the Mortimers. It was an impressive space, with a chandelier hanging from an ornate high ceiling, lavish floral wallpaper, rich oil paintings depicting rural idylls, and a marble floor.

Hill returned.

"Lord Mortimer will see you in the sitting room. He's with Mr and Mrs Mortimer. May I take your cardigan, Mrs Forbes? And your jacket, Lady Jane?"

Jane handed her jacket over for Hill to place on a coat rack in the corner, but Kate decided to hang on to her outerwear.

"Allow me to show you through. Miss Ursula thought it best to let you meet her grandfather and parents without her involvement."

Kate understood. Poor Ursula wanted her father's name cleared, but perhaps was a little squeamish when it came to discussing his fondness for Rebecca.

A few moments later, they entered the sitting room. It was the epitome of elegance, with two large sofas of patterned green and beige woven fabric either side of a stone fireplace, pale mint walls, and dark cream curtains that were tied back to let in the abundant September sunlight.

Here, they were greeted by Lord Mortimer and his cigar-smoking son Teddy, who both rose from their seats.

Lavinia, who remained seated between them, was smoking a cigarette in an elegant holder and seemed put out by their arrival. Even so, she instructed Hill to bring them coffee and dainties.

"Please take a seat," said Lord Mortimer, indicating the vacant sofa opposite. "I understand you're on some kind of mission."

"Oh, hardly that," said Kate, as she and Jane plonked themselves down as directed.

"Only, I'm aware of Ursula having a bee in her bonnet," said Lord Mortimer as he and Teddy sat down again.

"Yes, well, she did draw our attention to the matter of the christening – and how it would be ruined should gossip lead to your son attracting unwanted police attention."

"Just to be clear," said Teddy. "I'm perfectly ready to assist Scotland Yard in any way I can. But I'd like to do so as a willing member of the public, not as a suspect in a murder inquiry. I'm sure you understand."

"Did you enjoy the walk here?" Lavinia asked out of the blue.

Kate was a little taken aback, given the gravity of the subject under discussion.

Jane beat her to a reply.

"We did. It's a lovely day and a lovely estate, Mrs Mortimer. It reminds me of some of the finer estates I've visited."

"That's very generous, Lady Jane. I'm sure it pales in comparison to your father's. He's the Earl of Oxley, is he not...?"

"Yes, our seat is in Northamptonshire, although we spend most of our time in London."

"You live in London? How exciting. May I ask where?"

"Berkeley Square in Mayfair."

"Wonderful. I love to visit Harrods when I get the chance. They say one can buy anything there."

Jane laughed in a kindly way.

"I have to say they've always risen to the challenge whenever I've popped in."

Harrods? Kate was appalled. However, before she could change the subject, the butler rolled in a trolley load of coffee, butter shortbread biscuits, and iced sponge dainties, which he proceeded to set out on the coffee table between the sofas.

Unsurprisingly, only inconsequential chatter ensued while they tucked into their treats, but Kate wasn't about to leave it at that. She waited. And then, as Lord Mortimer took a sip of coffee, she pounced.

"Lord Mortimer, how would you describe your relationship with Rebecca Shaw?"

He seemed surprised, even to the point of almost scalding his tongue on the coffee.

"There was no relationship."

"You must have got to know her quite well though. She lived under your roof for almost a year."

"Hmm, well… let's say she was a good egg. Between you and me, I think one or two of the men in the village took a shine to her. That Enright fellow for one."

"Aubrey?"

"Yes, he had quite a thing for her. I'm not saying it's suspicious, but you'll no doubt make of it the same as I do – that he's a worthwhile port of call if you're keen to find out what happened to Miss Shaw."

Lavinia sighed.

"May I remind everyone that it's my granddaughter's christening next weekend. This is a lot of fuss we could do without."

Kate noticed that Lavinia had suddenly adopted a convincing tired look. It was as if she'd just finished a shift unloading sacks of sugar from a ship rather than having stayed in bed till ten before being driven to and from the church.

"Teddy," she begged.

"Darling, I'm sure our guests can see how exhausting things are for you." He turned to Kate and Jane. "Perhaps you could go easy on Lavinia. She's been overdoing it lately. All in a good cause, but she will insist on the fullest possible role."

Kate suppressed her preferred response, which might have questioned exactly what poor Lavinia had undertaken. Perhaps choosing which shoes to wear was more onerous than Kate had thought.

"Mrs Mortimer… I know a hard worker when I see one, but the quicker we learn the facts, the sooner all this can be resolved."

"That's all very well, Mrs Forbes, but can you resolve it by Friday? We have some very fussy in-laws coming to stay and I simply cannot deal with this at the same time."

"I'm sure we'll make some useful progress long before then."

"You don't understand. I'm already deeply involved in overseeing their arrival and the business of getting them settled in. Then there's the entirely different challenge of entertaining them."

"Yes, absolutely."

Ursula gave a polite cough from the doorway.

Lord Mortimer grinned.

"Come in, my dear. How's the little treasure?"

"Nanny's just bathed her. She's sleeping now."

"Nanny or baby!"

"Both."

Lord Mortimer laughed but Ursula looked quite serious as she came to sit with the investigators. Kate was pleased. This matter required Ursula's involvement.

"I couldn't help overhearing just now, Mother. The fact is Father won't be at the church next Sunday if he's arrested for murder."

Lavinia waved it away.

"It won't come to that. Right, Mrs Forbes?"

Kate shrugged.

"I hope not, but we really need your co-operation. For example, you said you liked Rebecca, but we've heard a conflicting report. It's the kind of thing that hampers any chance to get at the truth."

Lavinia hesitated for several seconds… before letting out a sigh.

"Alright, it wasn't a warm relationship." She flicked cigarette ash into a glass ashtray on the table. "One doesn't like to speak ill of the dead, so I thought it best to suggest a friendly relationship, that's all. The fact is I neither liked nor disliked her."

"And what about you, Mr Mortimer?" said Jane. "We've heard you were having an affair with Rebecca."

Teddy's eyes widened.

"Nonsense. I barely knew her."

"Are you sure?"

"This village gossip is appalling. I can see why Scotland Yard might come calling."

"It's not true then?"

"Lady Jane, you have my word. There was no affair. Rebecca Shaw simply did her job and then, as luck would have it, she secured an opportunity to better herself in New York."

"She left in a hurry though?" said Kate.

"The decision to leave was made late in the evening. She took off early the next morning."

"On foot?"

"Yes, to catch the train. She didn't want a fuss, and it's always been a perfectly safe route."

Kate wondered. If the rumour was true, covering up an affair would be a clear motive for murder. However, any chance of pursuing the matter was cut off by the appearance of Hill the butler.

"My Lord, there's an Inspector Ridley from Scotland Yard seeking an audience."

Fourteen

While the atmosphere in the sitting room was laced with anticipation, Lavinia Mortimer seemed the most ill at ease. Was that a look of dread etched into her features? Kate suspected so.

"Inspector Ridley," the butler proclaimed from the doorway.

The man from Scotland Yard entered and nodded to all. Whether he was delighted or annoyed at Kate and Jane's presence, he hid it well.

"Good morning and thank you for seeing me. I just have a few questions, if you don't mind."

"Not at all," said Lord Mortimer. "We appreciate you giving up your Sunday to look into this unfortunate business. Please do take a seat."

Ridley did so, beside Kate.

"You must have some coffee, inspector," said Lavinia.

"No, I'm fine, thank you."

"We have butter shortbread biscuits and iced sponge dainties. Please help yourself."

Ridley glanced at the coffee table in front of him.

"That's very kind, but no, thank you."

Teddy smiled benevolently at his wife before addressing Ridley.

"Inspector, how can we help?"

"This is strictly a police matter, so I'd appreciate some time with yourself and any of your family who might be able to assist me."

"Yes, I see." Teddy stared at Kate and Jane. "Ladies?"

Taking the hint, Kate checked her watch.

"Goodness me, is that the time? Inspector, we appear to be under your feet."

She rose from the sofa, as did Jane – but the latter addressed Teddy Mortimer directly.

"Before we go, just one question if I may?"

"Yes…?"

"If Rebecca Shaw was leaving in a hurry on foot, what became of her belongings?"

Not for the first time that morning, Teddy's eyes widened.

"Ah… yes… her belongings. That's a little awkward."

Jane turned to Ridley.

"The decision for Rebecca to go was made late in the evening. She left early the next morning on foot to catch a train from Upton."

Ridley wasted no time in addressing Teddy Mortimer.

"Lady Jane has asked a reasonable question, Mr Mortimer. I'd appreciate an answer."

Teddy nodded.

"The thing is… we were going to send them on."

"To where, exactly?"

"We gave Rebecca enough money to go to America. The idea was that she'd start a new life there. We never heard from her again though."

Ridley seemed frustrated.

"Let's see if I've got this right. Rebecca Shaw left here early one morning with a carpet bag and set out on foot for Upton railway station."

"Yes, that's right."

"Following the direct route, she wouldn't have gone through the village."

"No."

"So, as far as you knew, she took a train to…?"

"Southampton."

"Right… and she was going to contact you from there?"

"Yes, once she had a hotel address, we were to send her things on. Then, she'd get the next available boat to New York."

"But you never heard from her."

"No, we assumed it was down to us having given her enough money to start again with new things."

"We were very generous," Lavinia added.

"Enough for first- or second-class travel?" Ridley wondered.

"Third," said Lord Mortimer.

"And the clothes?" said Jane.

"Lavinia handled that," said Teddy. "They ended up in Upton – given away to the poor."

"Yes," said Lavinia. "It seemed the right thing to do."

"Right," said Ridley, "let's not detain Mrs Forbes and Lady Jane any longer."

"Quite right," said Kate. "We'll be on our way."

Ridley also stood.

"I'd like a quick word, if I might."

He followed them out to the vestibule where Jane retrieved her jacket, and out to the gravel drive at the front of the house.

"Just to remind you – you're not investigating this case. You're here on an archaeological dig. I know you've assisted me before, and I'm grateful, but please keep out of it."

Kate watched him head back inside.

"Well, that's told us, Jane. The thing is… Inspector Ridley might not be swayed by village gossip, but I fear there's so much of it, he'll have trouble getting to the truth."

As they made their way down the drive, they spotted someone by the gates.

"Ah, Dennis Wells," said Jane. "Gossip suggests he doesn't like taking no for an answer."

"Hello, ladies," he called as they approached.

"We'd like to ask you something," Kate called back. "If you don't mind."

"About what?"

Kate waited until they were almost upon him.

"The Enrights are spreading malicious gossip," she said. "We thought it might be useful to hear the truth from someone in the Mortimer camp."

Dennis frowned.

"There's not much to tell. I've heard the rumours and they're not worth a light."

"What about yourself. Did you know Rebecca Shaw well?"

"Not really. Our paths crossed but that's not surprising."

"Did you take a shine to her, Mr Wells."

"Who told you that?"

Kate saw anger flare in his eyes.

"Mr Wells, the better we understand the situation, the more likely it is we'll be able to help Teddy Mortimer."

He considered this for a moment.

"I told the police… I didn't know her well, but she was a nice girl. Always had a smile. Not just for me, for anyone.

She was good with the children. Kept them busy so they wouldn't get into trouble with their mother."

"Was that likely?"

"Mrs Mortimer suffered from terrible headaches, so she couldn't spend much time with them."

"Headaches? So, Mrs Mortimer didn't engage with anyone else then?"

"Well, she usually recovered enough for parties, fetes and what have you."

"I see. And now the children are grown up?"

"Oh, she's fully recovered now. She can have them to tea and to dinner. No sign of those headaches at all. Praise be, eh?"

"Yes, indeed. Praise be. Is there anything else you can tell us?"

"I've told you everything I know."

"Then we're grateful. Thank you."

He came past them, heading for the house. But as they reached the gates, he stopped and called.

"The man you should be talking to is Aubrey Enright. I clearly recall him having heated words with Rebecca before she went away. That is... before we *thought* she went away."

"Do you know what was said?"

"No, I couldn't hear it. Just his raised voice... very heated, it was."

They thanked him again and watched him head off.

"What do we make of that then, Jane? Heated words?"

"Let's not forget that Mr Wells is loyal to the Mortimers."

"Hmm, more malicious gossip? How do we think Mr Enright will react when we ask him about it?"

Fifteen

Standing at the gates to Mortimer Hall, Jane squeezed her aunt's hand.

"Are you glad you came?" she asked.

"To Penford? Yes, of course."

"I did say it would be an interesting weekend, didn't I?"

"You did."

Jane sighed.

"Just think, the original Norman gatehouse was sited right here."

Kate looked at the ground around her, and back to Mortimer Hall... and then the other way to the priory ruin.

"It's vandalism."

"Well, I'd imagine the gatehouse would have been a ruin too."

"Hmm, I suppose so."

They began their stroll along the medieval route accompanied by birdsong, a slight breeze and the sun in their faces. For Kate, it wasn't a matter of believing in ghosts, but there was a calmness about the place, as if it had been blessed.

"Who else might we consider for murder?" Jane wondered, somewhat bursting the spiritual bubble.

"Anyone associated with the original dig has to be looked at," said Kate.

"Including Lord Mortimer?"

"Aubrey Enright would no doubt settle for that."

"Lord Vincent Mortimer," Jane mused. "Eighty now, but sixty then. Did he kill Rebecca or pay someone to do so to preserve the family's reputation?"

"Possibly. Then we have the vicar. He organized the original dig, but he wasn't enthusiastic about the current one. Or is that down to Lord Mortimer's decision to allow an expert to take charge?"

"I would think so. After all, we can't suspect the vicar, can we?"

"You're right, Jane. That would be the end of civilization as we know it. Equally, if Lord Mortimer was keen for the new dig to go ahead, he's unlikely to be the killer either."

"True... who else then? Professor Nash?"

"A young Peregrine Nash. I'm sure he's not a killer."

"I'm sure you're right, Aunt."

Kate was glad. She didn't like the idea of Perry Nash being a secret homicidal maniac.

"There were other students here, of course."

"Two of them, but they would have worked together – and they were billeted at the church hall. Unless they crept out very early one morning... it doesn't seem likely though."

"What about Horace and Victor Enright?"

Jane gasped theatrically. "You heard what Aubrey Enright said. They're respectable men! One runs a furniture shop in Brighton, the other works for a brewery in London."

"They can't be ruled out."

"No," agreed Jane.

Kate thought some more.

"There was also Will Jessup. He did some digging."

"Yes, he did. Let's consider that. He was a labourer who also helped the former landlord of the White Horse Inn. He would have been available for a spot of cash work, and the team needed dozens of trenches dug."

"Speaking of the White Horse," said Kate, "we also have Betty Bagnall. She came up here with sandwiches and refreshments at least a couple of times. Then we have the delightful Cecily Cooper warning everyone about no good coming from disturbing the dead. I wouldn't want to bump into *her* on a dark night." She then thought of the man in the ill-fitting jacket and mismatched trousers. "And let's not forget Jim Archer delivering groceries on his bike. I wonder if he was out early that morning?"

By now they had reached the edge of the dig site, where Harry Gibson was first to come over and greet them.

"I hear you're investigating," he said, seemingly delighted by the idea.

"Yes," said Kate, "but right now we're thinking of the serene spiritual atmosphere here."

"Oh… right. Well, you've heard all the stories of greed and slackness, but this would have been a place of contemplation. I'm sure they weren't all selling supposedly miraculous objects to the sick for profit."

Perry Nash came over to join them.

"Hello there. Did I see you coming from the hall?"

"Yes, Inspector Ridley's there asking lots of awkward questions."

"Those poor Mortimers. Er… he doesn't suspect me, does he?"

"No, of course not, Perry. But if anything at all about your 1908 visit holds a clue…?"

"I've already told you what I know. I was much younger, much fitter, and my only interest was trying to please the vicar with a worthwhile archaeological discovery. As for Rebecca – I only saw her a couple of times when she brought the two young children for a look. Apart from that… nothing comes to mind."

"Are you staying long?" Harry asked.

"Not in my Sunday best," said Jane, indicating her clothing.

"Ah…"

"Besides," said Kate. "We're about to have a meeting with Aubrey Enright."

"Yes," said Jane. "Not that he's expecting us."

Sixteen

By the time they arrived back at the White Horse Inn, the lunchtime session was underway. Their target, Aubrey Enright, was already inside, leaning against the bar and talking quietly with Sid Allen and Will Jessup.

Perfect, thought Kate. The task now was to get him to answer their questions. Her growing experience in these matters suggested it might best be achieved by appearing to be completely uninterested in him.

"Jane," she whispered, "get your drawings out. We'll pretend to be fascinated by them while we sip lemonade at that table over there."

"I think you mean *despite* our fascination for my drawings we'll keep an eye on you-know-who."

"Apologies – that's what I meant."

Betty Bagnall called to them from behind the bar.

"It's warm, isn't it? Can I get you something? A refreshing lemonade?"

"Lovely," said Kate. "Thank you."

"Do you want them here or in the garden?" Betty asked.

"Oh, er…"

"It does get busy out there, mind. Lots of rough talk and that. Probably best here."

Kate looked around the spacious first-class lounge with its open windows.

"Yes, we'll stay here. There's a lovely breeze."

While Betty got their drinks, they considered the matter of getting Aubrey Enright to talk.

"Does he have a favourite subject?" Kate wondered as quietly as possible.

"Yes, the Mortimers," said Jane.

As she opened her sketch book on the table, laughter at the door heralded the arrival of Jeremy and Owen, who spotted Kate and Jane and came over to join them.

Owen was quick to admire Jane's drawing of the coin's two sides.

"How did that end up in a dead woman's bag," he wondered. "That's the question."

"Lemonade for two," said Betty, appearing at Owen's shoulder.

Jane covered the drawing with her hand, but perhaps too late to hide it.

"Interesting," said Betty. "Is it gold?"

"Yes," said Owen.

Kate might have ticked him off, but it seemed more sensible to caution Betty.

"Inspector Ridley and ourselves would prefer you not to talk about it."

"Ah right. Now, do you fellows want lemonade too?"

"Yes, please," said Jeremy for both of them.

As Betty went off, Kate gained their attention.

"You may as well know we're hoping to get that man over there to talk about his involvement in you-know-what. So, bear with us."

"Ignore any nods and winks, you mean?" said Owen.

"Exactly. Now, Jane – how do we achieve our goal?"

"Via the landlord?"

"Good idea. Why don't you give it a try?"

Jane turned to face the bar.

"Mr Jessup?"

"Yes, my dear?"

"We were talking about the 1908 dig at the priory. You lent a hand at the time, digging trenches for the vicar."

"Yes, as I said, for cash. I was never swayed by the vicar's love of it, or his suggestion I do it for free. I'd lost my parents and had no one in Penford looking out for me. I worked."

"And you did well."

Kate watched for Aubrey to join in, but he said nothing.

"I must say Penford's blessed with some wonderful history," she said, without knowing which history she was referring to. "Do you think the local people appreciate it?"

"Of course we do," said Aubrey. "We're not heathens."

Kate smiled. *Gotcha.*

"We were discussing stagecoach inns yesterday," she said. "I learned quite a bit."

"Yes, well… there's quite a bit to be learned," said Aubrey, his tone softening a little.

"I see the White Horse has kept the class system," said Jane. "I know the stagecoaches introduced first, second, and third-class services, which was adopted by the coaching inns and the railways."

"Yes, we have a first-class lounge," said Will. "It makes a lot of sense as I get to attract the best clientele. I keep a very good public lounge too, mind."

"There's an old coaching inn near Bournemouth with four different bar areas," said Owen.

"In Salisbury, too," said Jeremy.

Will nodded. "Before the railways, there were times it was so busy here that overnight guests had to share rooms and even beds with strangers."

Kate shuddered.

"That's one tradition we're better off without."

Will laughed.

Kate was still determined to draw Aubrey Enright into revealing his involvement with Rebecca Shaw, but perhaps she had taken a wrong turn.

"Tell us about Jack Ramsey," said Jane, referring to the previous landlord. "What was he like?"

"He was a good man," said Will. "I used to help him behind the bar and he'd tell me stories about the old days. Mr Enright here married his daughter."

"Ah," said Kate, "and didn't Jack Ramsey open the grocery shop opposite?"

"Yes, a couple of years after he sold the White Horse," said Sid.

"We're an enterprising people, given the chance," said Aubrey.

Kate was still wondering how to get onto the relevant subject.

"How are you getting on with the Rebecca Shaw investigation?" asked Sid.

Kate smiled. That would do nicely.

"We're hardly investigating…"

"It's the Mortimers you should be looking at," said Aubrey. "There's no smoke without fire. Isn't that right, Will?"

Will looked hesitant.

"Well, I suppose they wouldn't be the first toffs to misbehave."

"You're dead right, my friend," said Aubrey. "I can't think what's holding the police up."

"You were there in 1908," said Kate, "assisting the vicar."

"Yes, I'm sure I've mentioned it before. I can't think why they've gone back."

"I heard you knew Rebecca," said Kate, "and that you had heated words."

This alarmed Aubrey.

"Who told you that?"

"Is it true?"

"No, it's not true. I'd recall it otherwise. I'd recommend steering clear of gossip."

"Of course, Mr Enright. It's just that it's quite a specific claim – that your words were heated."

"Yes, well, I may have said something untoward about her employers, and she might have taken exception to it. It was a long time ago though. I don't recall the details. The fact is, this unfortunate business of her death has nothing to do with me."

Betty came over with the extra lemonade.

"Here we are," she said. "Just the thing for a day like today."

Kate had the notion that the drinks had been ready awhile, but that Betty wasn't one to get in the way of Aubrey's line of fire. With Aubrey, Will and Sid now talking loudly about something else though, here was a new opportunity.

"Betty, how did you get on with Rebecca?"

"Oh, well... she was lovely, but what's that saying... ships that pass in the night. Not that we passed in the night when she... I mean I finished up my job there before she started. I hardly spoke two words to her after that."

"You worked at the hall again though."

"Yes, I was working evenings here, but I helped the Mortimers for a while after Rebecca left. It was just for a few weeks until they got a new governess."

"I thought they kept you on?" said Sid, leaning out of one conversation and into another.

"Oh… as a housemaid, yes. I got on well with Mrs Mortimer, so I was kept on."

"You found a way to soften Lavinia Mortimer then?" asked Kate.

"I'd hardly say soften, but she liked to know what was going on in the village and for some reason seemed to think I was the best person to keep her up to date. I never said much, of course."

"And yet you left again."

"I came back here to help Will when he took over. Then my cousin Aubrey asked me to work for him."

"At Enright's Modern Grocery Stores?"

"Yes."

"Which Jim Archer and his wife now run."

"That's right – Jim and Anne. I helped them while the children were young."

"Then you moved on again?"

"Yes, I got a job in Upton. Then I came back to work here when Mrs Price passed away. To be honest, I prefer it here in Penford. I'm getting too old to be walking there and back."

"So, going back to Rebecca – you believed she'd left to live in America."

"Yes, which I thought was exciting. And that's it. Until you found the body, I don't suppose I'd given her a thought in fifteen years."

"I see."

Kate wondered if they were being harsh in considering her as a suspect.

"Would you be interested in sandwiches?" Betty asked. "The bread's fresh."

"Oh, yes please."

An order for ham and tomato all round was placed. Betty then seemed set to depart – but she leaned in close to Kate.

"I'll be finished in an hour. Come and see me at home. The first cottage on the right down Beehive Lane. I might have some useful information for you."

She smiled and left them, but Kate had her doubts.

"I don't know about you, Jane, but the last thing I need to hear is yet more gossip."

Seventeen

A good while after Kate and Jane had finished their lunch, Aubrey bade all farewell and departed.

"Time, gentlemen, please," Will called to the few remaining customers.

While licensing hours were relaxed for guests, the law demanded he remind anyone else to drink up and get out. As if to emphasize the point, Betty took out a tin of beeswax and began polishing the top of the wooden counter.

"I think it's time we took the air," said Kate.

"Good idea," said Jane, rising from her chair.

Kate glanced across to Will Jessup behind the bar polishing a wine glass while Sid Allen stared into space. She wished them both good afternoon and went outside with Jane.

"How about we have a word with Jim Archer?" she suggested.

He was across the street, in an alley between the grocer's and the post and telegraph office.

They arrived at the top of the alley, taking him by surprise as he broke up a crate.

"Oh, ladies. This one's rotten. I'll rescue what I can to make a new one."

They strolled halfway down before stopping.

"Mr Archer, we have a few questions, if you don't mind?"

"What about?"

"Rebecca Shaw."

"I do mind then. I'm not too keen on answering questions."

"Did you like her? Perhaps you took a shine to her?"

Jim looked set to flee inside. Kate needed to act fast.

"We might be outsiders, Jim, but we've worked with the police before. For example, we know you believe that Lavinia Mortimer despised Rebecca."

"I told that to Frank Drake."

"Constable Drake, yes. As I said, we do occasionally work with the police to take inquiries in different directions. We have no official role, but we report directly to Inspector Ridley of Scotland Yard. Your refusal to answer a few simple questions will only result in them being asked at the police house."

Jim considered it for a moment.

"I liked her, that's all. I was just a silly boy though. It couldn't have gone anywhere."

"Did you kill her?" Jane asked.

The question stunned him.

"No… no, of course not. It's Lavinia Mortimer you should be questioning. Either her or her father-in-law."

"More gossip, Jim?" asked Kate.

"No, I hate gossip. Sick and tired of it, I am. I run a shop and I mind my own business. I have responsibilities. Did you know I'm a husband and a father of three?"

"No, I didn't," said Kate.

"There's a lot you don't know. I'm an honest man. I've brought my kids up well. Our Sarah's sixteen and in service in Chichester. Our Freddie's just turned fourteen and has started working at the mill. Our Davey's nine and doing well at school. We're a good, honest family, and we don't deserve to have fingers pointed at us."

"Of course not. I completely understand."

"The gossip needs to stop before it does real damage."

"I agree, Jim. So, what's this about Lord Mortimer then?"

"Oh… well, his lordship was a bit strange back then. I mean his wife was alive, but he took an interest in Rebecca."

Kate hardly liked to ask, but she had to.

"What kind of interest?"

"Well, one minute he was fussing over her, the next he wouldn't speak to her. That's what I heard."

"Who from?"

"Rebecca."

"Right… that's quite something. Can you tell us more?"

"That's all I know."

They left Jim Archer to his chores and returned to the street.

"A word with Inspector Ridley?" Jane suggested. "We ought to let him know what we've heard."

Eighteen

Kate and Jane crossed the street and ventured up to the police house, where Kate spotted the inspector through the window with Constable Drake and Sid Allen.

They went in but had to wait while Sid finished his appraisal of the situation.

"It's all true. No word of a lie. I've seen it with my own eyes."

"I can't go and arrest Lord Mortimer because you say he's pretending to be old and frail. And for the record, Mr Allen, I'm not in the habit of listening to witnesses with a strong smell of beer on their breath. In my experience, alcohol leads to exaggeration."

"I'm only doing my duty."

"Good day, Mr Allen. Thank you for your report."

Sid muttered something under his breath as he left but there was no inclination from any quarter to find out what.

"Mrs Forbes, Lady Jane... to what do I owe the pleasure?"

"Tea?" asked a voice from the other room.

Mrs Drake duly appeared.

"Ah, no thanks, Mrs Drake," said Kate. "We won't stay."

"Righto, if you're sure. Give me a shout of you change your mind."

Once she had gone, Kate answered Ridley's question.

"Information. Jane and I have heard things."

"I did ask you to keep out of it."

"Jim Archer," said Kate. "You ought to know he says Rebecca Shaw herself told him of an intense interest coming from Lord Mortimer."

Ridley shook his head.

"You're not suggesting Sid Allen's telling the truth."

"He's probably not," said Jane, "but you'll want to keep all your avenues of inquiry open."

"Well, thanks for letting me know."

"We might have more later," said Kate. "Betty Bagnall has something for us."

"The chief gossip?" questioned Ridley. "I'm not interested."

"You never know," said Kate.

"With respect, I've spoken to everyone and got nowhere. Rebecca Shaw was stopped on her way to the station. But why? A fiendish attack is now most likely, but who would have been around at that early hour? Jim

Archer, the delivery boy, is keen to blame both Lord Mortimer and Lavinia Mortimer – but was Jim himself the killer? Or was it Dennis Wells? Or one of the archaeology team who went there early? I've heard of an affair between Teddy Mortimer and Rebecca, I've heard of Aubrey Enright taking a fancy to her... and what of the motive? Did the Mortimers kill her to stop blackmail? Or was someone else frustrated at having their love thrown back in their face? Is it even true she was leaving for America? Honestly, it's been hard to pin down the details, let alone a motive. Twenty years on, there's no way to know."

"I take it you're withdrawing."

"Constable Drake will continue to make inquiries. Hopefully, he'll turn up some new information. There are still a couple of Enrights to be questioned so that might lead somewhere. As for me though – I've got important business back in London. A deadly attack."

"Oh?"

"Greenfly on my roses."

A car pulled up outside.

"Ah, the chap from Upton with my ride."

Kate wondered where that left herself and Jane.

"Good luck then, inspector. Until next time..."

"Next time?"

He left the police house for Upton, while they headed back to the White Horse Inn.

"That was a fairly detailed appraisal by the inspector," said Jane. "He sounded fed up, but it didn't stop him being thorough."

"I suppose we're done," said Kate. "Are you still leaving tomorrow?"

"Yes, I'd like to get away by mid-morning. Things to do."

"Ah well, a twenty-year-old mystery... I suppose it was always going to be beyond us."

"I might just change into my fieldwork gear," said Jane. "But perhaps a glass of lemonade beforehand...?"

"Yes, alright."

They entered the first-class lounge. There was no sign of Will Jessup, but Jane went to wait at the bar all the same. Kate was halfway to a table.

"Aunt? We can sit at the bar."

"Oh, yes, alright."

Kate took Sidney Allen's usual perch and almost rested an elbow on the bar just as he always did, except Jane stopped her from doing so.

"Dust," she pointed out.

"Hello there," called Will as he came through the arch. "Just been watering the plants. What can I get you?"

"Two lemonades, please," said Jane.

"Righto."

"Are you a keen gardener?" Kate asked.

"I like to keep the plants watered in warm weather. Up the Royal Oak, they've got wilting shrubs. I mean, honestly, it doesn't take much effort to keep things going, does it."

"Inspector Ridley's off back to London. He's got greenfly to contend with."

"Nasty," said Will. "No good for the roses, that's for sure."

He served their drinks then excused himself with a need to check on the temperature of his beer barrels.

"I wonder what Betty was going to tell us?"

"Now, now, Jane – Inspector Ridley was quite clear about us accumulating yet more gossip."

"I know, but how about we finish our lemonade and pop over there anyway? You never know…"

Nineteen

Kate and Jane got as far as the church when they saw Jim Archer heading towards them on a delivery bicycle with an empty wicker basket on the front.

He smiled as he approached.

"You're busy for a Sunday, Jim," said Kate.

"Just running an errand. All done now."

It seemed strange. One minute he was breaking up a crate, the next he was whizzing about on his bike.

They continued past the church, stopping at the War memorial – a tall stone cross in the church grounds. Here, they offered a silent prayer for those local men who fell during the 1914-18 conflict. Ronald Lambert's name was among thirty from the combined parish of Penford, Upton, and the neighbouring hamlets.

Beehive Lane was the first turn on the left after the church. Heading down it, they were afforded a view into the orchard that ran along the back of a few old cottages up on the right. The first of these was set back from the lane. It had whitewashed walls, small paned windows and a slate roof.

"This looks like the place," said Kate.

She led them up to a royal blue door and rapped on the iron knocker.

"I hope this isn't going to be a baseless diatribe against Teddy Mortimer," she whispered.

A few moments passed without a response, so Kate knocked again. Hopefully, Betty wasn't putting the finishing touches to tea, as Kate was already at her limit for food and drink.

"Mrs Bagnall? It's Kate Forbes and Lady Jane Scott."

No reply came.

"She must be out," said Kate.

"Strange," said Jane. "She specifically asked us to call."

Kate pushed the door. It creaked open. Perhaps some oil in the hinges wouldn't go amiss.

"Mrs Bagnall?"

There was a large bag of flour on the floor just inside the short hallway, but nothing else to see.

"Mrs Bagnall? You asked us to call."

She felt uneasy. Should they go in? Weren't they just meddling? What if they were inside when Betty came back? Might she think they had overstepped the mark? Then again, what if she'd been taken ill?

Kate had an itch – and it needed scratching.

They stepped into the hallway and halted outside an open door on their left. Inside was a small, tiled fireplace with an oval mirror above it. The walls were a faded cream, the curtains faded yellow. There were two worn brown fabric armchairs, one padded with extra cushions. Apart from that, the room was empty.

"Let's try the back, Jane."

It was only a couple of steps to the back room, where they found a dresser full of crockery, a gate-legged table, a cushioned chair, a painting of St Peter's church on the wall, a geranium on the windowsill, and a large kitchen knife protruding from the back of a blood-stained body on a sizeable, patterned rug.

Kate gasped. Her heart thumped. There was a sudden need to sit down. But she remained standing. This was clearly a murder scene and evidence could easily be destroyed by carelessness.

She beheld Jane, who had a steely look on her face. Any emotions bubbling up were being held in check.

"Poor Betty," she said.

"Yes, Jane. Poor thing."

Kate sighed, both to calm herself and to prepare for the move beyond inertia. Someone had stabbed Betty Bagnall and…

"Jim Archer," said Jane.

"Yes, Jim Archer. Let's see what we can learn before we summon the police."

Jane stepped back to take in the scene.

121

"Alright… the rug in front of Betty has rippled up, as if she dragged herself eighteen inches or so to her bag and purse by the armchair." She bent down and peered at Betty's closed hand. "She's holding something." She prised a couple of fingers open. "It's a penny."

"How strange," said Kate. There were more pennies on the rug. "A robbery?"

"Possibly, but her attacker failed to make sure she was dead, which makes me wonder if they were disturbed."

"There's blood on the handbag, Jane. And the purse too."

"Yes, she used her last ounce of energy to get a penny from her purse. It must mean something."

"Alright, we've dallied long enough. Why don't you run and alert Constable Drake. And if you see Jim Archer… be careful."

Once Jane had hurried off, Kate took in the utter silence of the room. It felt a little spooky, but this was a time for clear thinking. Perhaps she could come up with a theory?

There was a box of candles on the table.

And what looked like a new cream woollen shawl.

There were also two apples and a pear in a bowl.

And a roll of bright yellow paper.

She moved to the cramped scullery, which was evidently used for cooking and little else. The larder cupboard had a few everyday items.

She felt a sadness. Betty was someone who bounced around in life, going wherever the winds of fortune blew her and never complaining. Yes, she was an undoubted source of gossip, but she was hardly alone in whiling away her spare time speculating about what other people got up to.

It was a full five minutes before a rush of activity at the front door evolved into the presence of Jane and Constable Drake.

"Oh, poor Mrs Bagnall," the latter groaned.

"Did you telephone Upton station to stop Inspector Ridley?"

"Yes, he'll be back. Lady Jane mentioned you passing Jim Archer on the way here. We'll obviously look into that."

"Betty has a penny in her hand," said Kate. "Jane spotted it."

Constable Drake looked down to the piece of possible evidence.

"Right..."

Kate continued. "She'd been mortally wounded but her final act was to get to her purse."

Drake looked up with a frown.

"I wonder why?"

"If Betty knew something, it's lost on us," Kate added.

"Did you take a look out the back?"

"No, we haven't."

They followed the constable to the unbolted door and out onto a small, paved area that abutted the fenced garden and the orchard beyond it.

"Interesting," he said. He was pointing at the stub of a cigar on the ground just ahead of them.

"It looks like one of the Cuban brands Teddy Mortimer smokes," said Jane. She knelt to check without touching the potential evidence. "The label says... *Romeo y Julieta, Havana.*"

Kate eyed the back fence. It was only three foot high. Anyone could have got over it. Including Teddy Mortimer.

"Right," said Drake. "I'll go and wait at the end of the lane for the inspector. I don't want him complaining he couldn't find the place. You two – please don't touch anything."

Twenty

Waiting with Jane for Inspector Ridley's arrival, Kate paced the floor in Betty's front room.

"Jim Archer…"

"Yes, Aunt, Jim Archer."

"Well, let's face it, Lord Mortimer couldn't have killed Betty. He can barely walk. And as for killing and hiding the first victim, he was keen for Professor Nash to come back and dig."

"Agreed," said Jane.

"So, Jim Archer…"

"A possibility."

"And Teddy Mortimer."

"Another possibility. The cigar stub is definitely the sort of thing he smokes."

"But Jane, doesn't it seem stupid to kill someone and leave your cigar at the scene?"

"Yes, it does."

"Unless someone's trying to pin the blame on him?"

"Possibly."

"Or what about this, Jane. Teddy did the deed himself and is making it look like he's been set up by someone else."

"We shouldn't rule anything out, Aunt. We saw Jim Archer coming from this direction. If he's our killer, then placing the cigar stub here would offer up a Mortimer to the police."

"That would certainly get Aubrey Enright's approval."

"And Jim is, of course, an Enright on his mother's side."

"He also works for Uncle Aubrey."

Kate's pacing had brought her to the front window. There was no sign of Ridley and Drake coming up the path though.

"Could Aubrey himself be the killer?"

"Possibly, although Betty was his cousin."

"Yes…" Kate turned to face her niece. "But what if she found out that Aubrey killed Rebecca and was about to give the game away? What's the life of a close relative compared with a fear of the gallows?"

"There's definitely a pattern, Aunt. It's just not quite visible yet."

"Yes, a pattern…" Kate began pacing again. "Two murders, twenty years apart. How do we connect them?"

"For now, it might be best to keep them separate in our thinking. Any common points will show up soon enough."

"Quite right, Jane. Clear thinking is what we need. The first murder then. Lord Mortimer, Teddy and Lavinia knew that Rebecca was leaving. What if a blackmail theory is right? What if Rebecca's pay-off wasn't a parting gift, but the first of many payments?"

"It's a possibility."

"It's a strong motive, Jane. If Rebecca was about to burden them with a lengthy campaign of blackmail, killing her would have got rid of the problem in one go. You're not convinced though."

"Ignore me. Something's wrong, but I can't put my finger on it."

"The second murder then. Did Betty have proof of an affair between Teddy and Rebecca? Was she about to blackmail him?"

"Again, it's possible, but why ask to see us?"

Kate paused by the door to the hallway.

"Yes, that's a good point."

"We need to dig deeper, Aunt."

Kate peered into her niece's troubled features.

"Yes, we do need to dig deeper. Much deeper. The two murders are linked, Jane, and we need to look into those who had the opportunity to be on the scene for both. For now, it's probably best that we don't let Inspector Ridley know what we're up to." Kate noticed that Jane's eyes had widened with a degree of alarm. It could only mean one thing. "He's behind me, isn't he."

"What's going on?" Ridley demanded.

"Inspector," said Kate, turning as her heart thumped. "I didn't hear you arrive."

"That's because I came in the back way. Drake informed me of the cigar stub so I wondered if the killer might have come over the back fence."

"Yes… well…" She could hear footsteps at the front.

"That'll be Constable Cartwright from Upton."

"Ah, reinforcements, good. As I was saying, you potentially have Teddy Mortimer's cigar and our sighting of Jim Archer not too far from here. I expect they'll be keen to explain themselves when you catch up with them."

"Yes, and the sooner the better. Constable Drake will take your statements and I'll have some questions for you once I've caught up a bit more with this latest unfortunate event."

"I thought Jane and I might be able to assist you."

"Mrs Forbes, I can't have you playing a role. Especially now the killer in our midst has struck again."

"I disagree," said Kate.

"Oh really?"

A uniformed policeman appeared behind him – Cartwright, obviously – but Kate wasn't put off.

"Yes, inspector. We should put our heads together and go over what we know about the here and now, and also the past."

Ridley frowned.

"On that basis, we might as well form a committee."

"That won't be necessary, inspector."

Ridley didn't look happy. He even said so.

"I'm not happy. This murder took place twenty minutes ago, not twenty years ago. That means there's a dangerous individual out there and they're not afraid to act."

"At least we can rule a few out," said Kate. "Those 1908 students who aren't here, Horace and Victor Enright, Ronald Lambert who died in the War, Lord Mortimer on account of his frailty…"

"Betty Bagnall wanted to tell us something," said Jane. "It very likely put her in harm's way."

Ridley sighed. "Look, I don't mind sharing a thought or two. I'm not a boneheaded outsider who assumes he always knows best."

Kate nodded. "If a Mortimer bumped off the governess to prevent blackmail, then might they have bumped off Betty because she was going to tell us what she knew of the matter."

Just then, Constable Drake reappeared.

"I've had a good look round, sir. I can't find anything of note."

"Alright, constable, stand easy."

"What do you think of the penny?" Jane asked.

"Yes, Constable Drake mentioned it," said Ridley. "I suppose it might be symbolic. Money, perhaps?"

"I'll ask around," said Drake. "See if it means anything to anyone."

"No," said Jane.

"No?"

"With respect," said Jane, "I'd suggest withholding information about the penny."

"Any particular reason?" Ridley asked.

"I can't explain it right now, but it might be important."

"I hid news of the gold coin for a good reason. I didn't want treasure hunters getting busy at the priory. But a penny?"

"If you announce that Betty's last act was to get hold of a penny, it might mean something to the killer. It might allow them to act to their advantage while we're still trying to understand its significance. There's also Aubrey Enright's story – that the Mortimers think they can treat people as badly as they like as long as they put a few pennies in your hand. There are a few pennies on the floor in there. Whether Betty meant to grasp more than one, we can't say."

Ridley nodded. "Alright then. Drake, Cartwright – not a word to anyone about the penny."

"Yes sir," both responded.

"Right," the inspector continued, "I'm going to have a word with Jim Archer and Teddy Mortimer. I have a feeling one of them is our killer. Cartwright, keep any busybodies away from the crime scene and make sure this place is gone over with a fine-tooth comb."

"Yes sir. We usually contact Chichester for this kind of thing."

"Alright, Drake, you get on the telephone to them."

"Yes sir, although it *is* a Sunday."

"I know it's a Sunday, constable. Just explain to them as politely as you like that a very grumpy inspector from Scotland Yard is working today, so would they mind getting their backsides here as quickly as possible."

"Yes sir."

"I'll interrogate Archer first. He's not as clever as Teddy Mortimer so perhaps I'll get lucky first time."

A few moments later, Kate and Jane left with Ridley and Drake, but they soon came to a halt on the widest part of the lane where a silver Alvis two-seater motor car was parked.

"I borrowed it from a chap in Upton," Ridley explained. "Drake, take it back to your place and wait for me there. I'll escort these ladies back to the White Horse Inn where they'll stay while I go to see Jim Archer."

They remained in step with the inspector all the way there.

"Back again?" Will asked from behind the beer taps once Kate and Jane were safely inside. He was taking bottles from a crate and placing them on a shelf.

Kate took a breath before stepping right up to the bar counter.

"I love the smell of beeswax," she said by way of passing the time.

Jane came up alongside her while they let Will finish his task.

"Right, ladies…?" he eventually said.

"Bad news, I'm afraid," said Kate. "It's Betty Bagnall. She's dead."

Will took half a step back.

"No… are you sure?"

"Unfortunately, Jane and I found the body."

"I can't believe it," he uttered. "What happened?"

Jane explained it as best she could, which hardly alleviated his state of shock. Meanwhile, Kate glanced away to the front windows. Across the street, the absence of Inspector Ridley outside the grocer's store most likely meant he'd been invited in.

This gave her an idea.

Twenty-One

It wasn't a conventional arrival at Mortimer Hall. Coming along the lane from the village allowed Kate and Jane to use the side gate, from where they heard raised voices from the back of the house. While propriety demanded they should ignore it and head directly to the front door, the business of investigation had a greater pull.

Creeping around the side of the building, Kate was first to the bushes on the corner. From there, it was plain that Teddy and Lavinia were just inside the nearest room – their disagreement billowing out through the open window into the rear garden.

Was this a bad time to kick an empty metal watering can?

Kate cursed the gardener for leaving it there, but now, with Hill the butler out the back like a shot, Kate grabbed Jane's elbow and led them in a hurry to the front door. Even as they ran, she was practising the look of frustration she would give Hill on his no doubt tardy journey back through the house to the front door.

As it was, he came up behind them.

"Ladies?"

"Ah, Hill, are you going to announce our arrival?"

Hill shrugged and pushed the front door open.

"Perhaps you'd care to wait in the vestibule?" he intoned.

While Hill went off, they once again admired this grand hallway. This time, Kate noticed the chunky stone door surrounds.

"I wish they would hurry," she said. "The inspector will be here once he's finished with Jim Archer."

It took a few minutes before they were greeted in the sitting room by Teddy and Lavinia. Although everyone was smiling as they sat, Teddy's eyes had narrowed slightly, suggesting a hint of confusion.

"Sorry for the delay, I've only just got back," he said. "I was checking on some fence repairs we're having done. It's good to do it on a Sunday when the workers aren't there. One can have a proper look."

Lavinia didn't bother to make any excuses.

"Have you returned with news?" she asked.

"Unfortunately, yes," said Kate. "It's Betty Bagnall. We found her dead."

"Oh my…" said Teddy.

"Bagnall…?" said Lavinia, her vague expression suggesting she'd never heard of her.

Jane was quick to help.

"You'll recall she was your children's nanny before Rebecca Shaw's time as governess. She also worked here again in a domestic role."

"Ah, yes... *Bagnall*," Lavinia said with a kind of shallow reverence.

Just then, Ursula came down to join them, but her cheery disposition vanished on being told the news.

"This whole thing is becoming really horrible," she said.

"Are you able to say what happened?" asked Teddy.

"Unfortunately, Betty was stabbed with a knife," said Jane. "We have no idea of the killer's identity, but you should know a *Romeo y Julieta* cigar stub was found near the scene."

Teddy didn't react at all.

"Isn't that your brand?" she prompted.

Now he understood.

"What are you insinuating?"

"Nothing," Kate assured him. "It's just that the police will view it as suspicious."

"They're imported Havana cigars. I buy them in London." Teddy went to his cigar case on the sideboard and studied the labels. "I have two brands... *La Aroma de Cuba*... and *Romeo y Julieta*."

Lavinia huffed. "Teddy was smoking at the church. Anyone could have picked up a cigar stub."

Kate shrugged.

"What about you, Lavinia? Were you anywhere near Betty's place earlier?"

"No, of course not."

"So, you haven't left the house?"

"No, I… well, I went out, but just for an afternoon walk. I often do. But as for Betty Bagnall, I always knew that gossiping tongue would get her into trouble one day."

"Inspector Ridley's due here soon," said Jane. "I'd advise you to tell him everything you know. It might alleviate his suspicion. I'd include the true story of your dealings with Rebecca Shaw in that."

"There were no dealings beyond our professional arrangement," said Lavinia.

"Of course," said Jane. "Perhaps we should leave, Aunt."

"Yes, I think we should," said Kate. "There's nothing we can do to help here."

"There was no affair," said Teddy. "I must stress that in the strongest terms. However…"

"Yes?" said Kate.

"My wife feared it might have developed into an affair. The word she used was… inevitable."

"So, the governess had to go?"

Lavinia nodded. "Yes, I wanted her gone. And for the past twenty years, I assumed that's what had happened."

Kate wondered if to believe her. Lavinia had a motive. Who was to say she hadn't had the means and the opportunity?

A noise at the door heralded the arrival of Lord Mortimer.

"Ah, returning guests!" he enthused. "Just the thing to rouse me after a nap."

They waited for him to take a seat before Lavinia relayed the latest news. He took a moment to digest it.

"That's awful," he said. "The poor woman."

Kate felt sympathy for him, but they needed to make some progress.

"We believe Betty's death is linked to Rebecca's," she said. "We think Betty might have known something vital."

"Oh?" said Lord Mortimer. "You think someone silenced her?"

"In a nutshell, yes. Inspector Ridley is thinking along the same lines. No doubt, he'll make it known when you see him."

"I'm not sure we can tell him much."

"We know about Teddy's fondness for Rebecca… and that there was a concern it might develop."

Teddy waved a hand dismissively.

"I must stress again that there was no affair. I'm an honourable man. I gave her money. She left to take up a position in America. There's nothing else to tell."

"Lord Mortimer? Do you have anything to add?"

"Teddy knows his own business. He's the one who can tell you if that's everything, not me."

"Then we'll say good afternoon."

Kate rose from her seat thinking that Teddy Mortimer was somehow blocking the investigation. Perhaps Inspector Ridley was right in suspecting him of murder.

Twenty-Two

Kate and Jane took the old priory path from Mortimer Hall up to the dig site, but there was little time to enjoy the view or the birdsong. There were too many gaps in their knowledge of events relating to two murders.

"Hello," Perry called as they approached. "We thought we'd get on with our work. Obviously, we'll keep away from the crime scene."

Kate looked beyond him to where Harry and the students seemed to be looking for something.

"We've lost a shovel," Perry informed them.

"Unfortunately, there's been another murder," said Kate.

"No…" Perry's mouth remained open; his brow crinkled with concern.

"Betty Bagnall," Kate added.

"The lady from the White Horse?"

"Yes, Jane and I found her at her cottage."

"You and Jane?"

"Unfortunately, yes," said Jane.

"Are you alright?" Perry asked. "I mean shouldn't the pair of you be somewhere comfortable recovering from the shock?"

"We're fine," said Kate. "A little shaken up, but we're both determined to find out who's behind it."

"Are you sure you're alright? I could walk you back to the White Horse…"

"Honestly, it's not necessary, but thank you for thinking of us."

"Yes, well… I mean, what were you doing there?"

"For some unknown reason, Betty asked us to pay her a visit. She said she had something to tell us."

"It hardly bears thinking about."

"We're short of clues, Perry. Is there anything you haven't mentioned relating specifically to Betty? Either twenty years ago or in the past few days. Any little thing might help."

"No, but let's ask the others."

It didn't take long to check with Harry, Jeremy and Owen on their recent encounters with Betty, but it failed to reveal any previously overlooked information.

"Thank you anyway," said Kate.

"We'll finish up what we're doing," said Perry. "I think this project will have to be closed down earlier than planned."

But Kate's attention was drawn to a figure by the ruin. The low sun in her eyes made it impossible to say who it was.

"A spirit…?" she wondered.

Jane squinted.

"It looks more like Cecily Cooper to me."

Kate sighed.

"What is that woman doing prancing around the ruin?"

"Let's find out," said Jane, striding forward.

Kate and Perry quickly followed.

"Hello?" called Jane. "Mrs Cooper?"

Cecily held her tongue until they were almost upon her.

"Let the spirits sleep in peace," she urged.

"We will," said Jane. "The team has almost finished its work."

Cecily seemed surprised and then somewhat satisfied.

"I see. Well… that's all to the good then."

Jane then explained Betty's death, which, predictably, shocked Cecily.

"Argh," called Jeremy from fifty feet away. "A fatality."

Kate shuddered.

"Who?" Perry called.

"The shovel."

"What?"

"It's face down in this trench with a broken neck."

A relieved Kate Forbes eyed Cecily.

"Well, I think we know who the killer was on this occasion."

*

Wandering back towards the village, they spotted Dennis Wells on the Mortimer estate boundary.

"I wonder if he knows," said Jane.

Kate waited until they were much nearer.

"Mr Wells? Have you heard – there's been a second murder."

He looked surprised.

"What? Who…?"

"Betty Bagnall."

"Betty? Are you sure?"

"Yes."

"Who'd want to kill Betty? She wouldn't harm a fly."

"We think she knew something about Rebecca's murder. The killer from 1908 might have struck again to stop her."

Dennis let the news sink in more fully.

"Dear old Betty."

"It's just a theory at this stage, but someone had a motive to get rid of her."

"It's true she knew a thing or two."

"Such as?"

"I don't know any particulars, but she usually knew what was going on and who was involved."

"Were you anywhere near her cottage earlier?"

"Me?"

"Yes."

"No, I wasn't. I was on the estate looking for poachers. They don't think too much of the Sabbath as a day of rest. More like a quiet day to lay traps and get their business done. Poor Betty. You never said what happened."

Kate explained with only as much detail as necessary.

"Poor Betty," Dennis repeated.

A silence fell on them. What else could they say?

"Is there much poaching?" Jane asked.

"Quite a bit. There's a lot of big families with poor incomes. Wild duck by the river's a favourite. Especially when it floods. You get little ponds form."

Kate considered it. "Hence the phrase 'a sitting duck', no doubt."

"I suppose so," said Dennis, perhaps still preoccupied with Betty's passing.

"Have you lived here all your life?" Kate asked.

"Yeah, born not far away. My father worked on a farm. I was one of seven children, so I worked on a farm too before I worked for Old Tom, the previous gamekeeper."

"You're married now?"

"Yes, me and Iris tied the knot in 1910. We have three boys and a girl."

Kate smiled.

"Thinking about 1908 though... before you were married..."

"If you're asking about Rebecca Shaw and whether I had any intentions, the answer's no."

"The police will ask the same question."

"I've already spoken to the police."

"Yes, to say that Rebecca was a lovely girl. The real question is – did you seek a relationship with her?"

"I just told you. No, I didn't."

"Are you sure she didn't reject your advances?"

"With respect, ladies, I'm not answering any more questions. If the police want to come asking, let them. Good day."

They watched him storm off. To Kate, everything felt wrong. The sky was blue and cloudless. The sun was warm and welcoming. The countryside was quiet and calm. And yet...

"If Rebecca turned him down, do we think he'd have reacted angrily?"

"It's possible," said Jane.

"Yes, it is. And if he had a motive, he certainly would have had plenty of opportunity."

At a fair distance, Dennis Wells turned to face them again.

"It's Jim Archer you want," he called. "He was the one who had a fascination for Rebecca. He used to come by on that bike of his, delivery or no delivery."

With that, he resumed his getaway.

"Inspector Ridley should be arriving at the hall soon," said Kate. "By car, I'd imagine. Perhaps we should cut across the field to avoid him."

"You mean it's our turn for another crack at Jim Archer?"

"I do."

Twenty-Three

On returning to the village, Kate and Jane went directly to Enright's Modern Grocery Stores. Although the premises were closed for the Sabbath, Kate rapped on the door and peered through the window.

A moment later, a child appeared by the counter – a boy of eight or nine. He was almost dragged away by a woman in her mid-thirties – Mrs Archer, no doubt. Jim Archer then came past them to stare. He looked pale – but whether it was due to worry or fear was impossible to say.

"Mr Archer? Could we have a word?"

He seemed uncertain of his next move.

"Jim? Come on, open up."

"I've already spoken to you." His voice was just about audible through the glass.

"This is important."

"We're closed on a Sunday. This is Mr Enright's shop. If you have anything to say, talk to him. Providence Cottage in Elm Lane. I have nothing to say to you."

"Now listen, Jim," said Kate. "I'm assuming Inspector Ridley has spoken to you about what happened."

Jim Archer said nothing.

"Jim? We know the inspector spoke to you."

"I… I explained everything to him. I still can't believe she's dead."

Kate sympathized. She couldn't be sure of his innocence though.

"Jim… I'm sorry it was us who told the police, but we couldn't overlook the fact that we saw you cycling back from that direction. If our roles were reversed, I'm sure you would have done the same."

He took a couple of steps closer, coming to a halt just short of the door.

"I've explained it all to the inspector. I left some flour round there. I thought she was asleep after work. He's perfectly satisfied."

"There's more," said Jane. "A witness says you had a fascination for Rebecca. You used to come by Mortimer Hall on your bike, delivery or no delivery."

Jim drew the bolt and opened the door. He looked angry.

"Who told you that?" he demanded, his voice now loud and clear.

"Never mind that," said Kate. "Is it true?"

"Teddy Mortimer wouldn't have known, nor his wife or his lordship. They never ventured round the tradesman's entrance. The only ones still there from all that time ago are the butler, the housekeeper and Dennis Wells."

"It doesn't matter who told us. Is it true?"

"It matters to *me* who told you."

Kate decided to change tack.

"Jim… you must know Penford as well as anyone who lives here."

"Better than most, I'd say. People don't look around them. They don't take much interest. They're too busy working, see. Then, when they get some time, it's too easy to listen to what others say about people instead of learning the facts for themselves."

"Penford seems a friendly place though. I'm sure it's just a few who spread all the nasty gossip. I'm sure many are firm friends who would do anything to help each other."

Jim softened. "Yeah, that's true."

"You grew up here. You must have endured hard times in the past."

"Everyone has those, lady. Well, most. No offence."

"None taken," said Kate.

"I hope you don't mind me asking," said Jane, "but how did your uncle Aubrey end up with a shop here?"

"Well… when Will Jessup bought the White Horse off Jack Ramsey, nothing changed for a bit. Then, a year or two later, Uncle Aubrey married Jack's daughter,

Margaret… it was his second marriage. He lost his first wife years before that. Anyway, he persuaded Jack to use his savings to open this place. I married Anne a couple of months after that, and he put us in to run it. That's how it came about."

"But you did grocery deliveries before that. When you were a boy."

"Yeah, the groceries were sold out of the White Horse back then. That room we use for darts."

"You seem like a decent chap. You have nothing to fear in telling the truth. Tell us about you and Rebecca."

Jim looked like that was the last thing he wanted to tell them about.

"You mean if I had a proper liking for her? If I went by there on the bike, delivery or no delivery?"

"Yes."

"You tell me who told you and I'll tell you if it's true."

Kate fumed. "This is ridiculous."

"It was Dennis Wells, wasn't it."

"Yes," said Jane, breaking the stalemate.

"Then he's a fool. Don't he know I saw him burning clothes?"

"What clothes?"

"Rebecca's clothes."

"Are you sure?"

"Yes, I'm sure. It was in 1908. I thought nothing of it at the time. Well, why would I? But now…"

"Why didn't you volunteer this information earlier?"

"I'm not too keen on Lavinia Mortimer, but I never had any problems with Dennis Wells, so I never said, for his sake. But if he wants to fight dirty by telling stories about me, so be it."

"This feud is ridiculous," said Kate.

"You think Dennis is just a gamekeeper? He does more than that. He acts as farm bailiff collecting rent. He don't mind getting physical if need be."

"We'll have to inform Inspector Ridley."

"Don't bother. I'll tell him myself. I wish you two would keep out of it. You're causing more trouble than you're fixing."

With that, Jim closed the door on them.

"Burning clothes," said Kate. "We must speak to Lavinia. But not right now. Aubrey Enright lives just around the corner. He'll want to know about Betty."

"Yes," said Jane, "assuming he didn't kill her, he's in for a shock."

Twenty-Four

A low thatched roof crowned Aubrey Enright's pretty, pale blue cottage. That much was evident well before Kate and Jane got close to it. Coming down the short leafy lane, they could see over the fence into the back, where a sizeable pig foraged beneath apple and pear trees. It was well known that the owner of a pig could obtain provisions by offering the animal's future meat as a form of payment.

At the dark red door, Kate rapped on the iron knocker. The interior would have traditional furnishings, she felt, with low ceilings and exposed wooden beams.

Confirmation of that would have to wait though as the look on Aubrey's face on answering her knock suggested they wouldn't be invited in.

"What do you want?" he asked.

Kate took a steadying breath.

"Prepare yourself for a shock, Mr Enright. Betty Bagnall is dead."

"What?"

His features suggested he didn't believe it.

"She's been murdered," Kate added.

"Murdered?" Aubrey seemed unable to get to grips with the situation. "How?"

"A knife. Jane and I found her."

"*You?*" Now he looked annoyed. "Why you?"

"She asked us to call on her. She said she had some information. We believe it's what got her killed."

Aubrey's shoulders slumped as he emitted a long sigh.

"Poor Betty… she was my cousin…"

"Yes, we know. You have our sincerest condolences."

"She was a good woman."

"Yes, indeed."

A lengthy respective silence followed. It seemed best to wait for Aubrey to break it.

"I looked up to her… when I was a boy. She was a few years older than me, see. No disrespect, but you ladies might have grown up differently. Life was hard for us. We got coal from the merchant in the station yard at Upton, but if we were short of money, the nippers had to push a cart there and back. Betty was always first to volunteer."

"That's a hard life," said Kate. "You would have all been living on the Mortimer estate back then?"

"Yes, living under their boot heels." He thought for a moment. "That said, I have many fond memories."

"I'm sure you do."

He stared into the middle distance, perhaps seeing it all again.

"You've done well, Mr Enright," said Jane.

"I have. The hard times are behind me. I'm very comfortable. Obviously, I'm on my own these days. I lost my second wife a few years ago. But I'm fine."

Jane nodded. "For those who aspire, you're an example."

His eyes brightened, leaving Kate to wonder if Jane had chosen the wrong career path. Wasn't the diplomatic service on the lookout for talented operatives?

"I try to encourage the young. I try to point the way."

"Indeed."

"But Betty… my dear cousin… she was someone I could rely on at the drop of a hat. Why would anyone want her dead?"

"We're working on the theory that she knew who killed Rebecca Shaw."

"That makes sense, I suppose."

Kate smiled as best she could. This next bit would be awkward.

"I hate to ask this, Mr Enright, but you left the White Horse at two o'clock. Did you come straight home?"

Aubrey became defensive again.

"Yes… straight home. I would have got back here a minute or two later."

"Did anyone see you?"

"You mean do I have an alibi?"

"It's a sensitive subject, but yes."

Aubrey sighed.

"No, I don't recall seeing anyone. Sunday afternoons are quiet in Penford, as you'll have noticed."

"Betty left the White Horse at around ten past two. We believe she was attacked very soon after reaching home – around a quarter past two."

"Well, there you are then. I was here at the dining table enjoying a cold lunch."

Twenty-Five

Kate and Jane left Aubrey and made for Priory Street. On the corner, they encountered the vicar passing by in the direction of the church.

"Ah, ladies," he called. "I've just heard about Betty Bagnall."

"Yes, a terrible business," said Kate.

"It is, very much so. Unfortunately, I can't stop. I have an appointment with Ursula Camley."

"Ah, christening discussions."

They walked with him.

"Jane and I were the first to arrive at the scene."

"Oh, you poor ladies. We'll say a prayer this evening for Betty, so please do come along."

"We'll be there," said Kate. "I'm just sorry for the village. Betty was an Enright, which is bound to add yet more fuel to the Enright-Mortimer fire. Penford seems cursed to pull itself apart."

"It's part of my mission here," said the vicar. "You heard my sermon this morning. About unity?"

"We did," said Kate. "We also heard what started the feud."

"Yes, an accidental death a quarter of a century ago. I can understand it causing a stir for a time, but for it to still be impacting on village life today… well, it's a disruption we could do without, especially with both families blaming each other for Rebecca's death."

"And no doubt for Betty's death too," said Kate.

"Lord Mortimer's in the clear for Betty, at least," said Jane. "He doesn't possess the strength."

"I'd put him in the clear regarding Rebecca too," said the vicar. "As you know I dislike gossip, but I've heard talk of it being about protecting the family's reputation in some way."

"We've heard that too," said Kate.

"I came to Penford in 1898, so I've known Lord Mortimer for thirty years. In all that time, I've never got the impression he's overly concerned with reputations. I think you'll find his view is that no long-established family will be perfect. I think he quite likes having rotters and cads in his lineage. It reminds him to rise above them."

"I get that impression too," said Jane. "When Professor Nash mentioned the possibility of looking for the graves of the de Vere family, his lordship scoffed. He said he didn't want us wasting a minute of our time on an overprivileged mob who paid cash for a burial spot within the church walls."

Just then, a Bentley came along and pulled up by the gate. No sooner it had stopped, Ursula hopped out and instructed the chauffeur to wait.

Judging by her disposition, she was still in shock at Betty's death.

"I still don't know what to make of it," she said. "Poor Betty. She didn't deserve to end up like that."

"Absolutely," said Kate.

"And my poor father. He's now being lined up for two murders."

Ursula was crestfallen.

"Don't worry," said Kate, "Jane and I will continue to investigate. And perhaps you can help us."

"How?"

"We need more information about Dennis Wells. I know he's a loyal member of Lord Mortimer's staff, but he's been avoiding our questions. Someone on the inside might have better luck finding out how well he knew Rebecca Shaw."

"Question him, you mean?"

"No, I mean find a way to ask Lord Mortimer and your father about him. He may yet turn out to be the killer."

"Right, leave it with me."

"Good," said Kate.

"Have you spoken to any of the Enrights yet?" Ursula wondered.

"Yes, Jim Archer went to Betty's cottage but says he left a bag of flour there without going in. He thought she was asleep. As for Aubrey Enright, he says he was at home at the time of Betty's death."

"What time was that?" Ursula asked. "Just in case it helps me with Dennis Wells."

"A quarter past two."

"Right."

"Oh," said the vicar. "That's odd."

"What is?" asked Kate.

"I saw Aubrey Enright as I was coming back to the church earlier. That was at a quarter past two. I know that because I was meeting Mrs Bennett regarding evensong."

Kate took it on board.

"He lied, Jane."

"What now then?"

Kate considered it for a second or two.

"I'm sorry, Ursula, but we need to talk to your mother."

"Why my mother and not Aubrey Enright?"

"We'll speak with him soon enough, but we've only just seen him so we know his mood. He'll make an excuse. It might be best if we leave him until we can trap him. Right now though, there's the business of burning clothes, which is why we need to speak with your mother."

"I don't understand."

"Don't you worry. All will become clear. Now you stay here and sort out those important christening arrangements. We'll keep you informed. I promise."

Kate and Jane hurried off in the direction of Mortimer Hall, although, with the White Horse Inn on the way, the elder of the two could soon see beyond it to the police house and a silver car parked outside.

"Let's not walk all the way, Jane. My feet are killing me."

"No problem, Aunt. I'll drive."

Twenty-Six

The burgundy and black Triumph Super Seven roared through the open gates to Mortimer Hall, raced along the gravel drive, and skidded to a halt outside the front door.

"I've always wanted to do that," said Jane.

"Right," said Kate, "before Hill emerges with one of his looks, let's remind ourselves why we're here. We need to build a list of those we can set aside. That's the only way to get a good crack at identifying the killer."

Hill opened Mortimer Hall's heavy front door and gave them a look.

Kate waved.

"Hello again, Hill. I expect you're wondering why we're back."

"Not at all, Mrs Forbes. If you could wait in the vestibule, I'll alert his lordship."

"Thank you," said Kate, although she needn't have bothered because the words merely bounced off the butler's disappearing back.

"I have a feeling we're not welcome," said Jane.

"I don't care," said Kate. "I'm completely fed up with Mr and Mrs Mortimer. It's poor Ursula I feel sorry for, but we must make what progress we can while the trail is fresh. We've eliminated Lord Mortimer from our list of suspects. Let's see if we can do the same for Teddy and Lavinia, whether they deserve our help or not."

It was just a matter of moments before they were whisked into the sitting room, where Teddy and Lavinia were seated on opposite sides of the unlit fire.

"Back again?" said Teddy. He looked disappointed.

Lavinia looked set to add her disapproval, but all were interrupted by the arrival of Lord Mortimer.

"More questions, ladies?" said his lordship. "I think we answered enough of those with your friend from the Yard."

"Well, first things first," said Kate. "Jane and I can rule your lordship out of anything pertaining to Betty Bagnall's murder. And by extension, we can do the same regarding Rebecca Shaw's death."

"Now, now, ladies," he said. "I could have killed Rebecca. Don't forget, I was a fit young man of sixty then. I'm pretty nimble now, you know." He then gave a sad little laugh. "But no, I didn't kill anyone."

"Were you fond of Betty Bagnall?" Kate asked.

"Yes, very much so."

"And Rebecca?"

He paused to reflect.

"Rebecca… yes… I loved that young woman." This provoked a heavy silence with plenty of exchanged glances. It didn't last though. "Oh, not like you're all imagining."

"I'm sure we're not imagining anything," said Kate.

Lord Mortimer went to the window where he stared somewhere into the distance.

"You see, I never had a daughter. But if I had – she was the kind of daughter I'd have wanted."

Kate felt the truth of it, even before his lordship turned to face her with moist eyes.

"Back in 1908, I felt very much let down," he continued. "When Lavinia told me she felt Teddy was growing too close to Rebecca, I became angry. I believed Lavinia when she said we could nip an affair in the bud."

Lavinia nodded. "It wasn't an affair, but who knows where it might have gone had I not sent her away. That said, you must understand I had no ill intentions towards her. I just wanted her out of the house with as little fuss as possible."

Jane raised a finger to capture Lavinia's attention.

"Around the time she went missing, Dennis Wells was seen burning clothes."

Teddy looked shocked. "What clothes?"

"Rebecca's clothes," said Jane.

"You didn't know?" Kate asked Teddy.

"No…"

"It doesn't change anything," said Lavinia. "Rebecca never contacted us, so I asked Wells to get rid of some unwanted items. It's nothing sinister."

"Mrs Forbes," Teddy pleaded. "I made one mistake. I was attracted to Rebecca. It shouldn't ruin our lives."

"It's quite plain," said Lord Mortimer. "If you want to help us, you must find the killer."

"Ha!" said Teddy. "What with all this gossip going around, everyone thinks it's me."

"Aubrey Enright certainly dislikes you all," said Jane. "He says you think you can get away with anything as long as you put a few pennies in a person's hand."

"More foul words," said Lavinia. "It'll be one of his lot behind it. You'll see."

"That's what I was wondering," said Jane. "Do you keep household accounts?"

Lavinia looked puzzled.

"Why do you ask?"

"A list of deliveries during September 1908 might be helpful."

"We keep ledgers," said Lavinia, "but you're going back a fair while. They may have been thrown out."

"Could we check?"

"Mrs Allenby keeps track of things. She's not here, but Hill is."

Lavinia and Teddy left Lord Mortimer to his thoughts and took Kate and Jane down the hall to the rooms by the kitchen. One of these was the butler's pantry. Here, Lavinia took charge.

"Hill, we're looking for the ledgers relating to household deliveries."

"I have an excellent memory, ma'am. Perhaps I can assist. Is it a missing item?"

"Unfortunately, it's to do with this wretched business twenty years ago. Rebecca Shaw's death."

"Ah… then I'm not quite sure how…?"

Jane stepped in. "We were wondering if the grocery boy made a delivery on the morning she left."

"Ah, I see. Well, in September 1908 that would have been Jim Archer. Is there a specific date?"

"Wednesday the sixteenth," said Lavinia.

Kate glanced at her.

"The inspector had me check my diary," said Lavinia.

"Ah."

"Let me see…" said Hill.

He bent down at a low cabinet and checked through a number of ledgers.

"Ah… this one is 1895 to 1897."

"Why do we keep them?" Teddy asked.

"Because there's never been a directive to dispose of them, sir. If I might say, an acquaintance of mine is head butler at a house near Arundel. Their records go back to 1680."

"Gosh," said Teddy.

"Ah, here we are…" Hill stood up and proffered a dark blue volume. "1907 to 1909. If there was a delivery, it should be recorded here."

Lavinia took the book and handed it to Kate… who handed it to Jane… who sifted carefully through the pages.

"1908… September… the sixteenth." She looked up at the expectant faces. "A delivery of grocery items."

Twenty-Seven

Kate was spoilt for choice. Among a hundred or so parishioners leaving the church after evensong and prayers for Betty Bagnall, she and Jane found themselves a step behind the duo of Aubrey Enright and Jim Archer.

All Kate could think was – which one should we interrogate first?

Of course, they had already given Inspector Ridley a full update of their recent findings. Ridley, in turn, had asked them to stand down and leave it to him – which made it difficult to openly interrogate either of the suspects, especially as Ridley, Drake and Cartwright were standing by the lychgate smiling at them.

"A very moving service," said the inspector as the villagers filed past. He then lowered his voice for Kate and Jane's ears only. "Just to keep you up to date, Betty's body has been removed to the mortuary. We've also dusted for fingerprints, but I'm not expecting any joy on that front."

Kate said nothing – instead smiling at Teddy Mortimer, Dennis Wells, Harry, Owen and Jeremy as they passed by. Perry remained by the door, chatting with the vicar.

"Any plans?" Ridley asked once the rush had dissipated.

"No, just a quiet evening in the White Horse," Kate informed him.

"You'll be having sandwiches then," said Ridley.

"Yes... poor Betty Bagnall and her shepherd's pie are no more."

Constable Drake brightened.

"My mum's cooking something. I'm sure we could squeeze you and Lady Jane in."

"That's very generous, constable, but Jane and I are exhausted. It's rest we need."

"Of course."

They all left together, police and amateurs, discussing matters quietly as they walked the two hundred yards to the White Horse Inn with a number of suspects not so far ahead of them.

"I'll make more inquiries in the morning," said Ridley. "Ideally, one of them will have fled Penford. Then I can put out an alert and that'll be that."

"That's wishful thinking, inspector," said Jane.

"It's all I've got at the moment, Lady Jane. I've followed logic, but I still can't get to the killer."

"Teddy Mortimer's cigar stub," Constable Drake reminded them. "Let's not forget it was found at the second murder scene."

"Yes, very convenient," said Ridley. "It reeks of a set up. Either that, or Teddy Mortimer left it there to make it *look* like a set up."

"Don't give up," said Jane. "There may yet be other angles we haven't considered."

Kate noted Aubrey Enright going into the White Horse, while Jim Archer crossed the road for home.

A few moments later, Kate and Jane were stopping outside the inn, leaving Ridley, Drake and Cartwright to continue to the police house.

Aunt and niece remained by the front door until the three policemen had disappeared into Mrs Drake's aroma filled home.

"Right," said Kate. "Jim Archer."

They crossed the silent street and knocked. It wasn't possible to see through the glass due to pulled blinds, but it wasn't long before he opened the door to them.

"Ladies? Did you talk to Dennis Wells?"

"About the clothes? No, but we've told the police. We also spoke with the Mortimers. If Dennis was doing the burning, Lavinia would have given the order."

"It's a terrible business," said Jane. "Rebecca and Betty didn't deserve to die like that."

Jim looked sincerely worried.

"I don't know anything about either, I swear."

Jane pressed on. "We were looking into deliveries to Mortimer Hall back in 1908. You delivered groceries there the morning Rebecca left."

"Did I?"

"Yes, you did. These noble old houses keep records going back centuries. There's no mistake. You delivered groceries to their door that morning."

"If you say so."

"Be honest, Jim. You saw Rebecca, didn't you."

"Look, I'm busy. Sorry."

He tried to close the door, but Kate put her foot in the way.

"This makes you look guilty," Jane warned him through the shoe-width crack.

Silence fell, but Kate was determined to keep her foot in place.

"We're not the police," she said. "If you're innocent, let us help you prove it."

She waited, but the silence continued.

"Jim? Think of your family."

A further wait ensued before he pulled the door open again.

"Did you speak with her?" Kate asked.

"Yes, I said good morning."

"Is that all?"

"Not quite. I was surprised to see her leaving the house early with a carpet bag, so I asked where she was off to. She said the station. By that, she meant Upton."

"What happened after that?"

"Nothing. She walked off and I rode back to the village, which you'll know is in a different direction."

Kate wasn't impressed.

"Jim, you were with Rebecca just before she was murdered, and you were at Betty's around the time of her death."

His face was ashen.

"I'm no killer," he said. "You have to believe me."

Twenty-Eight

Kate and Jane returned to the sparsely populated first-class lounge of the White Horse Inn to be greeted by a surprise. Jim Archer's wife, Anne, was behind the bar. The business of running a pub and looking after paying guests hadn't stopped during the Great War, so Kate accepted that Betty's demise was no reason for the White Horse to do so now. It still felt a little jarring though.

Over in the far corner, Teddy Mortimer was having a quiet drink with Dennis Wells. On making eye contact with Kate, both raised their tankards. The ladies smiled and nodded.

"I think we've earned a nice peaceful Sunday evening, Jane. Let's try to enjoy it."

Aubrey Enright was at the bar, already halfway through his first pint of ale. He turned but failed to greet them.

"Hello, Mrs Forbes, Lady Jane," said Anne Archer. "I'm helping out for a bit."

"It's very good of you," said Kate. "Perhaps we could have two small dry sherries and some cheese sandwiches."

"Oh, but it's Sunday evening. Sandwiches won't do at all. How about a baked potato from the oven with melted cheese? Professor Nash and his students have already ordered two apiece. Be three-quarters of an hour?"

"Oh well… lovely. Thank you."

Kate guessed that Perry and the students were in their rooms. Even so, they would be down at some point, so she opted for the large table by the window to accommodate them all.

Just then, Sid Allen came in, greeting all prior to plonking his frame down on his regular stool at the bar. To Kate, his appearance was no surprise – unlike the arrival of an agitated Jim Archer a few moments later.

He spotted Kate.

"Is the inspector here?"

"No, he's at the police house, Jim."

"You don't need to talk to the police," Aubrey advised.

"Ignore him," said Kate. "Go to the inspector if you have something to say."

"Don't listen to them," said Aubrey. "The younger one's a titled lady. You know what that means, don't you – she's been on the Mortimers' side from the start."

"That's ridiculous," said Jane. "I'm a historian. I deal in facts."

"What facts?" mocked Aubrey.

"Alright, here's one for you," said Jane. "You were seen not far from Betty's cottage around the time of her murder. You told us you were at home."

Aubrey's face grew red.

"I don't recall you two being appointed constables, and you're certainly not detectives."

"You're right," said Kate, "we're neither of those. I'll tell you what we are though. We're two ordinary people with an interest in justice."

"Don't set yourselves up as morally superior. You're no more than a couple of interfering busybodies."

Kate felt that now would be a good time to take a gulp of restorative sherry, but Anne Archer was behind the bar with the two filled glasses on a tray – seemingly afraid to enter the bear pit.

"What is it you fear, Mr Enright?" Jane asked.

"Me? I fear nothing and no one. But I'll tell you this much for free – you can't go around ruining people's lives with your endless questions."

"Some might say that constantly accusing the Mortimers is designed to do just that – ruin lives."

"That's different. They're guilty. That's to say, at least one of them is. Now you back off."

"There's no need for threats," said Kate, wishing the landlord might take a stand.

"Mrs Forbes is right," said Jim Archer. "Keep it civil, if you don't mind."

"You be quiet, Jim Archer," said Aubrey. "And as for you, Mrs Forbes – just you leave it to the police so they can get the right Mortimer."

Teddy Mortimer rose to his feet.

"That's enough, Enright. You've gone too far – yet again."

"Ah! I hope everyone's hearing this. Let me tell you, Mr Mortimer, I have a seat on the parish council. Thirty years ago, your lot were chasing my father for rent. Your dad was the magistrate sitting in judgement in court and sending my cousin David to prison. And when my family was hungry, Lord Mortimer made sure we couldn't go after hares or rabbits, or fish or pheasants. Well, now it's changed. You might be a fellow parish leader, but you have nothing over me."

"That's a fine speech for a born liar," said Teddy.

"I'm no liar!"

"We've just heard it from Lady Jane. You lied about your whereabouts when poor Betty was murdered. How can you be both a pillar of the community and a liar?"

"I don't answer to you."

"Did you go to Betty's cottage?"

"No, I did not!"

Kate interrupted.

"If you went to see Betty, it wouldn't have been about anything pleasant. That could have been said here at lunchtime. Did she upset you, Mr Enright? Did you go there to berate and bully her?"

"That's his usual method," said Dennis Wells.

Aubrey shook his head.

"Dennis Wells is more likely to be the killer. He killed Old Tom so he could take his job. Everyone knows that."

Dennis was incandescent.

"You take that back."

"You're a murderer."

"No, I'm not! Ask Jim."

Jim Archer looked shocked.

"Don't ask me. I can't help you."

"You useless toad. Why can't you tell the truth for once?"

"Alright, I will – I saw you burning Rebecca Shaw's clothes."

This drew a few gasps.

"Gentlemen, please," said landlord Will Jessup, finally trying to calm them down. "Let's keep things respectful."

Just then, Kate spotted Harry Gibson on the stairs opposite. He had stopped halfway down, perhaps having second thoughts about enjoying a quiet evening in the first-class lounge. She signalled to him and pointed in what she hoped was the direction of the police house.

Harry nodded and made his way out.

Dennis meanwhile wasn't finished. His gaze was wholly upon Jim Archer.

"It was you who most likely killed her," he declared.

"I did not!"

"What did she say? Did she call you a silly boy?"

"No!"

Aubrey took several steps towards the Mortimer contingent.

"Jim's an Enright. He's no killer. It's one of you two, or that dangerous woman at Mortimer Hall."

Teddy took a step forward.

"I trust you're not referring to my wife?"

"Gentlemen, really…" Will Jessup appealed once again.

This time he gained a respite of sorts, although with Teddy and Aubrey just ten feet apart, tensions were still palpable.

Jane nudged her aunt.

"What was it you said about enjoying a nice peaceful Sunday evening?"

Owen and Jeremy then appeared on the stairs. They too looked as if second thoughts were uppermost in their minds. But Professor Nash appeared behind them and guided them through the battlefield.

"What on earth's going on?" he asked as they joined Kate and Jane.

"It's a fight," said Kate, "and we seem to have ringside seats."

"Oh," said Perry. "Do you think I should intervene?"

Kate watched Teddy and Aubrey begin to circle each other.

"Perhaps at the end, Perry, when they've knocked each other out."

Teddy suddenly lurched forward and grabbed Aubrey's collar.

Jim rushed forward and grabbed Teddy.

Dennis then leapt in and grabbed Jim.

Then Aubrey shook Teddy off and threw a punch that missed.

Teddy again grabbed Aubrey... who wriggled free to square up again... as Jim and Dennis wrestled each other to the floor.

The front door flew open... and in rushed Inspector Ridley and Constables Drake and Cartwright... just as Aubrey threw another punch... which again missed Teddy... and landed on the side of Drake's head.

The constable was momentarily stunned... but came back to life looking to thump Aubrey... just as Ridley grabbed the punch-throwing parish councillor and pulled him away.

"This brings back my days on the beat," was all the man from Scotland Yard could say.

Wondering where that left them, Kate signalled to Anne behind the bar that it might be a good time to serve the sherry.

Twenty-Nine

Jane sat on the edge of the bed in her aunt's room, while Kate sat in the corner on a small, padded armchair reflecting on the meagre fruits of their investigation.

"What do you think, Jane? Is it Teddy Mortimer? Or is it Jim Archer? Obviously, Aubrey Enright has to be a suspect too. And let's not forget Lavinia Mortimer. She wasn't there for this evening's fisticuffs, but she's acted oddly the whole time we've been here."

"I'm not sure, Aunt. Something's missing. Something that would bring sense and order to the information we have. It's just out of reach though."

"Alas, I fear it might stay there."

"It's no consolation to know that Inspector Ridley is facing the same problem. He might have interviewed people at different times and in different ways, but..."

"He still hasn't a clue?"

"It might yet fall on Teddy Mortimer," said Jane. "That gossip about him having an affair with Rebecca."

"Lavinia refutes that. She nipped it in the bud, remember? Unless she's lying. Then the potential for blackmail would loom over that particular episode."

Jane sighed. "We never promised Ursula that we'd prove her father's innocence, but I'm thinking he hasn't exactly helped."

"No, he hasn't."

"We need to step back a little, Aunt. Someone killed Rebecca Shaw for an unknown reason. Then that same person killed Betty Bagnall, because she was about to tell us what she knew. That's our theory in a nutshell."

"A nutshell with holes in it."

Kate stood up and began pacing.

"Essentially, we've missed something, Jane."

"Then let's go back to the start."

"To me finding the body?"

"No, before then."

Kate stopped pacing. "Nothing happened before then, Jane."

"Precisely."

"I don't follow."

"Think about it. All but the killer assumed Rebecca Shaw left Mortimer Hall for a new life in America... and for the next twenty years, life continued as normal. That's a tableau, frozen in time until you discovered Rebecca."

"Yes..."

"Let's concern ourselves only with any changes that have occurred since then."

"I'm assuming you mean however seemingly insignificant."

"Yes."

"Betty was murdered."

"Yes, but she was safe for twenty years until the discovery ignited a change. Let's follow that for a moment. What did she know?"

"Something relating to Rebecca, most likely."

"Yes, either something old that suddenly became relevant… or something new that she learned because of the body turning up. Either way, it had the potential to identify the killer."

"But how would the killer know that she had this piece of information?"

"Because Betty told them."

Kate felt the force of the observation.

"I'd suggest attempting to discover who Betty talked to – but I suppose that would be everyone."

"Most likely."

"But one of them reacted badly. Did Betty seek to blackmail a Mortimer? Or was she planning to turn Jim Archer over to the police based on something she knew. I'm thinking blood on clothing in 1908, which wouldn't have meant much at the time with Rebecca successfully starting a new life in America."

"There's just one problem, Aunt. And it's a problem that spoils every theory. Nothing explains the gold coin in Rebecca's bag and the penny in Betty's hand."

Kate puffed out her cheeks. "Remind me why that's important."

"Put yourself in Rebecca's place. How would you deal with owning a valuable gold coin?"

"Well, I wouldn't leave it rolling around in the bottom of my bag, that's for sure."

"What if it were in your pocket and a robber suddenly accosted you?"

"I suppose I wouldn't have time to do much about it."

"What about if you saw a robber up ahead? Would you take it from your pocket and drop it in your bag?"

"No, the robber would most likely grab the bag."

"What then?"

"With all that grass, I might drop it on the ground and keep walking. Let the robber have the bag. I'd come back for the coin once they'd gone."

"But this robber… they didn't take the bag. They didn't even take the purse."

"Then she was attacked for some other reason."

"Another reason, Aunt? A lustful man?"

Kate shuddered. "It has to be a possibility."

"Yes, but that horrible thought doesn't explain the gold coin in the bag or the penny in Betty's hand. Unless I've got it completely wrong."

"Oh Jane, you're testing me to the limit. But don't let that stop you. I want us to catch this evil brute."

"Alright, let's see. We know the killer struck a second time after twenty years. We think that's because Betty had put two and two together. We know she died with a penny in her hand. We believe it must mean something."

"But what? The Enrights have that phrase about pennies. Aubrey's quite passionate about it."

"Yes… 'The Mortimers think they can get away with anything as long as they put a few pennies in your hand.' But what if it was something else? Owen made a comment when I was looking at my sketches of the stater. He was wondering how it ended up in a dead woman's bag. Betty was there. She saw the sketch of the coin and asked if it was gold."

"Yes, exactly the question I would ask."

Jane smiled. "It's exactly the question most laymen ask about an archaeological find."

"It doesn't help us much though," said a frustrated Kate.

"We'll get there, Aunt. It's probably staring us in the face."

"I know, Jane. I know."

Kate went to the window and peered out over the moonlit landscape. A quarter of a mile away, the priory ruin was a ghostly presence.

"I'm just thinking about the priory legend, Jane… about hearing the monks sing."

"Unfortunately, I've not heard them, Aunt."

Kate turned to face her niece.

"They say it happens when there's a gentle breeze. It supposedly carries their song."

"Surely that's just the breeze they're hearing."

Kate retook her seat.

"I quite like the idea. It appeals to the poet in me."

"Aunt? You never mentioned having a poetic side before."

"I don't tell everyone, Jane. Actually, I don't tell anyone. The thing is, there are mysteries that the scientific mind cannot solve."

"True…"

"That's not to take away from academic research, Jane. After all, you're making a wonderful career in it."

A moment passed with Jane's features frozen.

"Jane? Are you alright?"

Suddenly, she came back to life.

"Constable Drake!"

"What?"

"The killer."

Kate gasped. "He can't be. He'd have only been twelve in 1908."

"Aunt, don't you remember? Constable Drake has a scout badge."

"A what?"

"Don't you see?"

Kate shook her head. "I wish I could, Jane. I really do."

"Then let me explain it to you…"

Thirty

On a sunny Monday morning, Kate and Jane were up at half seven.

"Breakfast and a good walk, I think," said Kate as they came down the stairs in functional daywear to the first-class lounge. "Get the heart and brain going."

Will Jessup was coming in through the arch from the other bar. He looked smart in a white and navy-blue waistcoat.

"Ah, ladies. I'm sorry you're leaving. I do hope you had a good stay. Apart from…"

"We've been well looked after, thank you," said Kate. "Despite everything, Penford's a lovely place to visit."

"I'm glad you think so, Mrs Forbes. Let's face it, if a born winner like Aubrey Enright is investing his wealth here, we should all be just fine."

"Indeed. I wonder if the inspector will be down for breakfast soon?"

"He's already gone out. Business at the police house."

"Ah."

As it was, Perry Nash, Harry, Owen and Jeremy were soon down to join them. It was a convivial last breakfast before the professor and his team's final poke around by the ruin.

By half eight, fuelled by porridge, coffee, toast and marmalade, Kate and Jane tried the police house – but Ridley had already left for Mortimer Hall. Mrs Drake invited them in to wait, but they declined.

"I always think better when I'm walking," said Kate as they headed west along Priory Street in the direction of St Peter's church. "Even if the porridge might be slowing me down."

"Me too," said Jane, coming to a halt.

"What is it? I said you shouldn't have had that fourth slice of toast."

"I'm fine, Aunt."

"You haven't changed your mind about the killer?"

"No."

A robin landed on the edge of the water trough just ahead. This was a raised stone bathtub which could readily be filled from an adjacent spring for the benefit of horses, cattle, sheep… and, quite plainly, birds.

"I sometimes wonder if the simple life isn't the way," said Kate, eyeing the robin.

"I love the simple life, Aunt Kate – especially when I've had too much of the complicated life."

"Well, let's keep walking. It might free our minds a little more."

Reaching the church, they spotted the vicar a little farther on by the War memorial. He seemed to be in quiet contemplation.

"Not long until the tenth anniversary," said Jane.

Kate considered a whole decade passing so quickly since the end of the Great War.

"No doubt the district will turn out to mark the occasion," she said. "I suppose we should say hello to the vicar. And farewell, of course. Let's wait by the entrance."

As they passed through the lychgate, Jane stopped to pick something up, which Kate could now see was a cigar stub. For some reason, Jane sniffed it.

"One of Teddy Mortimer's... and it's given me an idea."

"You're not taking up cigar smoking, are you?"

"No, Aunt... ah, the vicar."

Kate turned to see the reverend approaching.

"Good morning, ladies."

"Good morning," said Kate. "We're not disturbing you, are we?"

"No, no... I was just remembering the end of the War. Did you know we had a festival of peace here? We put up a marquee on the green and filled everyone's plates with pies, sandwiches, cakes... there was music... and the children had races for prizes. Then the men decided to race too. The Mortimers versus the Enrights. All animosity forgotten."

He checked his watch, which Kate noted.

"Don't let us hold you up, vicar."

"No, it's alright. I'm waiting for the bishop. He's staying with a friend in Upton, so he'll be here at nine on the dot."

"It sounds important," said Jane.

"Yes, he's under pressure to replace the three chapels in Upton with a new parish church. There's a strong mood there to have it in the larger community and relegate St Peter's in importance."

"Oh well," said Kate. "Times change, I suppose."

"They do, Mrs Forbes. St Peter's as parish church represents things as they once were, not as they are now. But I'm wittering. Perhaps you ladies have something else on your minds?"

"Yes, Rebecca and Betty. It kept Jane and me up late last night. The good news is that Jane may have solved it."

"Oh, good work, Lady Jane. Who's the killer?"

"Sorry, vicar, but I need to discuss it with Inspector Ridley first. He's popped out though."

"Of course. You know, it's a shame you can't solve this accursed feud between the Mortimers and the Enrights at the same time."

"Only they can solve that," said Kate.

Suddenly, Jane was nodding.

"Perhaps, in a very small way, we could help."

"Oh?" said the vicar.

"It's something Dennis Wells said… that Jim Archer could clear his name regarding the death of Old Tom."

The vicar nodded.

"An Enright supporting a Mortimer man? I'd consider that a ray of light for Penford."

Thirty-One

Jim Archer wasn't pleased to see them enter his shop. For Kate, this was the least surprising thing of the entire weekend.

"Unless you're here to buy groceries, I can't help you. Sorry."

"Could Dennis Wells be the killer?" Kate asked.

This clearly took Jim by surprise.

"He could be."

"Is he the type?"

"I don't know."

"Aubrey Enright says Dennis is a murderer. He says he killed Old Tom to get his job. The thing is, Dennis says you can clear him."

"I'm not sure how."

Kate smiled in what she hoped was a sad way.

"You know the truth. That's something you'll have till the end of your days. As for Penford... well, it'll remain as it is."

Jim seemed undecided about something.

"I was brought up to always tell the truth. I was also brought up to be on my guard against the Mortimers."

"It's a shame," said Jane. "Hiding the truth to please Uncle Aubrey will always hold you back as a man of character."

Jim Archer was a little taken aback by Jane's uncharacteristic personal slight. Kate though seized on it.

"Jane, we should leave. Jim Archer is clearly a man who needs his uncle's permission to speak the truth."

If Jim Archer had been taken aback by Jane's words, he was now appalled at Kate's.

"Is that what you think?" he gasped.

"It's what the entire village sees," said Kate.

They were set to turn, but Jim spoke.

"Dennis shouldn't have pointed a finger at me."

Kate had endured enough.

"Jim Archer, you sound like a whingeing schoolboy. While Penford cries out for men and women of honour, a small-minded tit-for-tat between the Enrights and the Mortimers offers only mean-spirited poison. I hope you can justify your part in it to your children."

Jim looked set to sound off again, but something changed in him – perhaps because his wife and son had appeared in the doorway behind the counter.

"Davey's about to head off to school, Jim," said Anne.

Jim ruffled his boy's hair. "You work hard, son. School's the best thing in the world."

Anne Archer nodded to the ladies before leading Davey away again, leaving Jim to gather his thoughts once more.

"Alright… Dennis got the gamekeeper's job because he was the meanest. The Mortimers had a lot of poaching problems and some of the workers were taking liberties. They needed someone who took no nonsense."

Jane nodded. "Dennis thinks you can clear his name regarding Old Tom's death. But Tom drowned in the river. You could only clear his name if you were there."

Jim stayed silent, so Jane continued.

"Were you poaching?"

"No, I wasn't."

"Were you working for the Mortimers then?"

Jim wouldn't say, which relit Kate's already short fuse.

"Jim Archer, I couldn't give two hoots for Aubrey Enright and his pompous opinion of himself – were you working for the Mortimers?"

Jim sighed. "Just a bit here and there. I know what you mean about Uncle Aubrey, but don't tell him. He'd make a right old fuss."

Jane stepped in again.

"You didn't take the feud seriously then?"

"No."

"Why not? It was Aubrey's uncle, so that's a relative of yours too."

192

"Yes, to me, Great Uncle Stanley. But horses kill men all the time. There was a bloke crushed by his own horse in Upton only two years back. So who knows what really happened."

"So, despite working for Aubrey in the new grocer's store, you continued to do occasional work for the Mortimers."

"Yes."

"And were you there when Old Tom drowned?"

"Dennis always wondered if I was on the other side of the river that day. I've always said I wasn't. The police didn't take much interest, nor the Mortimers, so he got the job and life went on."

"But you *were* on the other bank?"

"Yes."

"And you saw what happened?"

"Yes."

"But you said nothing in order to keep out of trouble with your uncle Aubrey?"

"Yes."

"Jim... did Dennis Wells kill Old Tom?"

Jim took a breath.

Thirty-Two

Leaving the grocer's, Kate and Jane spotted Inspector Ridley and Teddy Mortimer getting out of the borrowed Alvis outside the police house.

"Interesting," said Kate.

They hurried across the street and up to Ridley, who was waiting on the doorstep shaking his head at their arrival.

"Have you arrested Teddy?" Kate asked.

"Not yet. He's helping me with one or two questions I have."

"At the police house?"

"Yes, well, things are serious now. I believe Teddy was having an affair with Rebecca Shaw and that there's a possibility of blackmail on her part. Betty Bagnall no doubt knew something about it and had to be silenced. Then we have the cigar stub and the well-known Enright jibe about the Mortimers thinking they can do anything as long as they put a few pennies in your hand. It's possible Betty was trying to tell us exactly that."

"We might be able to help you," said Jane.

"Not now, ladies. I've got plenty to be getting on with. If you'll excuse me…?"

The amateur investigators made their way back to the White Horse Inn.

"We really need to talk to him, Jane."

"We will, Aunt."

Entering the White Horse, they said hello to Will Jessup who was polishing the tables.

"Teddy Mortimer's in the police house," Kate informed him.

"Oh? That's never a good thing."

"Unfortunately, one of his cigar stubs was found at Betty's," Kate added, wondering how long it would take for the information to get around.

"I see."

"Here's an idea, Aunt," said Jane. "Before we pack our things and leave, how about a final morning together? We could visit the dig site for one last look and then bring Perry and the others back here for an early lunch. Then I'll follow you back to Sandham."

"Oh?"

"I thought I might spend a day or two there… if that's alright?"

"Oh Jane, that's a lovely idea. Yes, let's do that. I must say, you've got it all worked out."

"Yes, Aunt."

Kate turned to Will Jessup again.

"If I'm ever in the area again, I'll come and stay here. You have a lovely establishment."

Will seemed to stand taller, perhaps with pride.

"My great-grandfather built the White Horse. It went downhill a bit when the railway came through Upton, but now? Order's been restored. Penford's not all about the Enrights and the Mortimers, you know."

A few moments later, Kate and Jane were heading along the cross-field track bound for the dig site.

"I'm assuming there's some sort of plan whirring away in your head, Jane?"

"Oh definitely, Aunt. In fact…"

Jane turned back to Priory Street. Kate followed. Two minutes later, they were outside the police house.

"Wait here, Aunt. I just have to ask Inspector Ridley something."

"Righto."

Jane vanished inside. A few moments later, she returned.

"To the dig site, Aunt!"

"What did he say?"

"Let's just say he was surprised but interested."

A little over five minutes later, they entered the sunlit pasture. Perry Nash waved and came to join them. Once again, he and Kate were wearing strikingly similar straw

Panama hats, which gave the latter a warm feeling... or was that just the sun?

"This is so lovely," she said, her hand outstretched to indicate the serenity of wildflowers, bees and butterflies, and the activity of students dressed for field work and sifting dirt in trenches.

"It is," said Perry.

Kate glanced at the weather-worn remnant of the priory church.

"A Cluniac priory," she mused.

"Yes."

"Dedicated to St Martin."

Perry smiled.

"That's right."

"So you'll be packing up soon?"

His smile dropped away.

"Yes, in an hour or two. Um... I ought to get back to Jeremy. He's trying to expand a trench."

"Of course. Don't let us stop you."

No sooner Perry had gone, Jane called Harry over. He came to join them, as eager as ever.

"Harry, your family lives in Redhill. What's that – a two-hour drive?"

"I suppose it is."

"Is your father at home?"

If Harry hadn't been puzzled before, he was now.

"No, he'll be at work in London, Jane."

"Does your mother drive?"

"No."

"Does anyone at home drive?"

"No, but our neighbour does. Mrs Welford. She's chairwoman of a million committees and she drives everywhere. She has a Vauxhall 20/60 cabriolet, if that helps."

"It does. Now here's what I'd like you to do…"

Thirty-Three

Around two hours later, just before lunchtime, Kate, Jane, and Harry were seated at a table by the window in the White Horse Inn. Jane particularly wanted to sit there for a clear view of Priory Street and anyone approaching by car from the east side.

Of course, she was under pressure for having invited a number of people there, citing Scotland Yard's approval. Hence, the general public were excluded with apologies to the landlord for his forbearance.

By the bar, were gathered the Enright contingent – Aubrey, Jim and Anne Archer, and friend of the family, Sid Allen. There might have been more. According to Ridley, a few other village Enrights had crawled out of the woodwork demanding to be present. The inspector wasn't having it though.

The Mortimers were present too. Seated in the far corner were Lord Mortimer, Lavinia, Ursula, and Dennis

Wells. Teddy remained with the inspector at the police house.

"What's the hold up?" groaned Aubrey, not for the first time.

Kate tutted and would have rebuked him, but just then, a pale blue Vauxhall 20/60 cabriolet with its top down came to a roaring stop just outside.

Jane was out there in a flash. Kate and Harry followed to see how all this might play out.

"I got here as fast as I could," said an excited Mrs Welford.

"I'm ever so grateful," said Jane, peering into the back of the car.

"When I heard that Scotland Yard needed me…"

"You're a marvel, Mrs Welford," said Harry. "I'll bring it inside."

"No, let me do that," said Jane. "I need you to do me a favour."

"Yes, of course," said Harry.

She whispered something in his ear, which sent him into the inn and up the stairs.

"Fingers crossed, eh?" said Kate.

She and Mrs Welford held the inn's front doors open so that Jane could readily get through with the equipment.

"Don't be alarmed," Kate told those inside.

Will Jessup was quick to come round from behind the beer taps for a closer look.

"It's a metal detector," Jane explained.

"A what?"

"It detects metal in the soil. Any metal at any depth. Even something small."

"Really?" Will looked amazed, as did everyone else gathered there.

Kate might have looked amazed too. Perry Nash had specifically said it could do no such thing. A huge wartime landmine a few inches under the soil, yes. But any small piece at any depth? Surely not. Except this was part of the plan.

"We've been waiting for it to arrive," Jane continued. "It's been at work at a dig in Hampshire all weekend. By all accounts, it was a great success."

Kate knew for certain that the machine had in fact spent the weekend in Harry's old bedroom, but she remained quiet on that point too.

"Apparently, they used them in the War," Jane went on. "To find mines. They're much more precise now, of course."

"Is it electricity?" Cecily Cooper asked at the open window – no doubt brought to the scene by her inquisitiveness – which might have explained three or four others gathering outside.

"Yes, an electrical battery powers it," Jane explained.

"Then you must not take it to the priory!" Cecily cried. "The electricity might wake the dead."

Kate's eyebrows shot up.

"I'm sure that's not true, Mrs Cooper!"

"We're not taking it to the priory," said Jane. "Inspector Ridley has commandeered it."

"What for?" asked Lord Mortimer.

"He wants to find something. He wouldn't say what, but he'll soon be alerting people to expect it on their property."

"He's not coming to my home with it," said Aubrey.

Kate shrugged. "No doubt the inspector will construe something from anyone who refuses permission."

Aubrey huffed. "Well, I wish he'd hurry up and get here!"

"I second that!" said Sid Allen.

"Oh, shut up," said Lavinia Mortimer.

Will Jessup shook his head. "Well, while there's a lull, I might just escape all this unpleasantness and water my plants."

"Could we try to keep this civil?" said Lord Mortimer.

"Quite right," said Kate. "We might not even need the machine if people answer the inspector's questions honestly."

As Will left, Anne Archer came out from the back to take over at the bar. This coincided with Perry Nash returning from the dig site. Of course, he knew of Jane's plan and had been sworn to secrecy.

Even so, he looked far too excited.

"Hello Kate. How are you this fine lunchtime?" he said in a manner that would have got him rejected by any self-respecting amateur drama group. "I've left Jeremy and Owen at the site for a last look."

Kate led him back outside.

"We can't do anything just yet. Jane has it all worked out though."

"Right, so, we just wait."

"Yes."

"Well… it's a shame we didn't get to talk about other things, Kate. Obviously, solving murders is more important, but… well… I'll be heading back to Oxford soon."

Kate felt a pull, although she couldn't be sure which kind.

"I imagine you have plenty of interesting projects awaiting you."

"Yes… plenty. There are still a couple of things of interest here, but I'll tell you once this is all sorted out."

A silence descended on them – one that Kate felt a strong urge to fill. But what with?

"Your name's quite interesting," she ventured, even though she had no idea why.

"Oh, it's quite common, really. It comes from the Middle English phrase, *atten ash*. It means 'by the ash tree', no doubt relating to a settlement."

"I meant Peregrine."

"Ah… yes, from the Latin – the traveller, the wanderer."

"That's very poetic. I shall think of you differently now. When you're happily ensconced in Oxford researching what-have-you, I'll imagine part of you longing to be outside, venturing to far-flung fields in search of adventure... or at least in search of old bones and bits of metal."

Perry laughed.

"I heard on the grapevine that Kate is short for Katherine – both lovely names."

"Thank you. I was at the British Library once with time to spare, and it occurred to me to look it up. Katherine is from the Greek. It means... leader."

"Well now... those Greeks certainly knew a thing or two."

She wished she could lead the two of them a bit more, but she was a widow of only fifteen months.

"Look, come inside and sit down, Perry. We'll have lunch in a while. No talking about you-know-what though."

As they joined Jane and Mrs Welford inside, Will Jessup returned.

"If anyone wants sandwiches, do let Anne know. We have a good range."

"No, thank you," said Lavinia Mortimer. "I've had almost more sitting around than I can bear."

"You're not the only one," said Aubrey Enright.

Just then Harry came down the stairs and headed over to Jane. Kate was watching as he leaned into her ear to whisper something.

Jane, in turn, whispered something back, which had him nodding and leaving the inn by the front door.

"Jane?" said Kate. "Is everything alright?"

"Yes, Aunt."

Thirty-Four

Kate looked around the first-class lounge. The windows were now closed to keep the public out of earshot. Inside, a number of fresh arrivals had joined them.

Inspector Ridley was standing by the fireplace.

Cartwright and another constable who had cycled over from Upton were stationed by the front door.

Teddy Mortimer was seated with Constable Drake.

Kate was happy to be at a table with Jane, Perry, Harry, Owen and Jeremy in the corner near to Ridley. It no longer felt like a pub though – more like a courtroom.

"This has been a difficult case," Ridley began. "Not least of all because of the animosity between the Mortimers and the Enrights. I want you to know that I never gave any credence to the gossip flying around unless it could be corroborated by evidence."

"I'm glad to hear it," said Lavinia Mortimer.

Ridley ignored her.

"I can now reveal some information you won't be aware of. Rebecca Shaw was found with a gold coin in her bag." This caused a murmur, but Ridley pressed on. "You also won't know that before Betty Bagnall died, her last act was to retrieve some pennies from her purse. One of them was found in her hand."

Aubrey gasped. "That's the Mortimers! That's what she's telling you. Cart 'em away."

"Be quiet," Ridley insisted.

"You have Teddy Mortimer," Aubrey pointed out. "Now finish the job!"

Ridley continued though. "An element of doubt has crept in. I want to be sure I'm right. Don't worry, it won't take long."

All around the room, gazes flicked from one person to another.

"Who's the killer?" Lavinia Mortimer demanded.

"We'll come to that shortly."

A degree of muttering bubbled up, to which Ridley raised a hand.

"The investigation led to more than one possible conclusion. I had to ask myself whether one or more members of the Mortimer family had disposed of Rebecca Shaw to prevent blackmail. This possibility suggested that Betty Bagnall knew about it and had to be silenced before she spoke to Mrs Forbes and Lady Jane."

"That's scandalous!" said Lavinia Mortimer.

"It sounds true to me," said Aubrey Enright.

"Nonsense," said Teddy Mortimer.

Sid Allen piped up.

"Betty spoke to Mr Mortimer. I saw them together yesterday at the church. She was putting pressure on him. A few hours later, she was dead."

Aubrey Enright nodded his approval.

"Betty's already told us – it's the Mortimers."

Jane interrupted. "What if the penny in her hand signified something entirely different?"

All eyes were suddenly on her.

"What?" Aubrey didn't like it at all.

"What if Betty wasn't threatening Teddy Mortimer with blackmail?" said Jane.

"But she was!"

"Betty was Ursula's nanny. I believe she saw past the feud to the fact that the young aren't part of it."

"This is nonsense!"

"Aunt Kate?"

"Yes, of course, Jane. Mr Enright, Betty upset you when she revealed she was giving a christening gift to Ursula's baby. That's why she was speaking to Teddy Mortimer at the church. That's why she was putting pressure on him. To let her do so despite Lavinia's coldness. That's why you went round to see Betty. To berate her."

Kate reached into her bag and pulled out a cream woollen shawl and a roll of bright yellow paper for wrapping it as a gift.

"Constable Drake retrieved it from Betty's cottage for me."

Aubrey looked down.

"I did go, but I changed my mind once I'd knocked. I left again. I didn't berate or bully her."

"The thing is," said Jane, "it's very likely that you, Mr Enright, disturbed the killer."

"Oh?"

"Let's turn elsewhere for a moment," said Ridley. "Jim Archer was an eighteen-year-old at the time of Rebecca's death."

"I'm no killer," said Jim.

"No? We've established that you were out on your bike at the time, doing deliveries and what-have-you. We've also established that you were fond of Rebecca."

"That's not a crime," said Aubrey.

"I've got nothing to hide," said Jim. "Yes, I liked her. We used to talk. Not for long, mind; she was always busy. But she was friendly."

"She was a woman with a bright future," said Ridley. "You were a delivery boy. Did she push you away that morning?"

"No!"

"Perhaps you got angry with her?"

"I never got angry!"

"Perhaps Betty Bagnall knew about it and was about to tell Mrs Forbes and Lady Jane. Perhaps, as an Enright, she couldn't turn you over to the police, but had chosen to let someone else do it."

"I never killed Betty, if that's what you're saying."

"Jim has a strong sense of right and wrong," said Aubrey. "He's no killer."

"And that's the truth!" said Jim.

"A Mortimer did it," said Aubrey. "Or they got their man to do it. Dennis Wells is no angel. He murdered Old Tom to get his job. It's a well-known fact."

"I did not kill Old Tom!" Dennis insisted.

But Kate's eyes were on Jim Archer. He looked agitated.

"Jim," she said, "I do believe you're an honest man."

"I am!"

"Then perhaps, as an honest man, you could tell us the truth about Old Tom's death."

All eyes were now fully on Jim Archer.

Jim himself glanced at his Uncle Aubrey before rising to his feet and settling his gaze on Kate and Jane.

"When Old Tom fell in the water, Dennis jumped in after him."

"You were there?" Aubrey was surprised.

"Yes, I was there doing some work for the Mortimers. I often did when I was short of money."

"But I was paying you to work for me!"

"It wasn't enough to live on, Uncle. It never has been. Sorry."

"Carry on," said Ridley. "You were short of money and doing a bit on the side for the Mortimers. What did you see?"

"I saw Old Tom fall in the water. I was further upriver on the far side checking for poachers' traps, so I had no chance to get to him. Then I saw Dennis jump in and drag him out. He tried to save him but he was too late. When Dennis looked up, I ducked out of sight. He always thought I was there. I always said I wasn't. He never killed Old Tom though."

Jim looked relieved to have got it off his chest.

"Thank you for telling the truth," said Kate.

"I've been wrong to hide it all these years, but Uncle Aubrey would have killed me for working for the Mortimers on the side."

Aubrey looked fit to burst. "You traitorous little rat. You're out of a job!"

Jim said nothing but he and Anne moved to seats further away before sitting down again.

Despite the bout of honesty, Ridley's gaze remained firmly on Jim Archer.

"Mrs Forbes and Lady Jane saw you leaving Betty Bagnall's house immediately after her murder."

"I've already told you – I took a bag of flour round to her, that's all. I called out but there was no answer. I thought she might be asleep after work, so I left it just inside the front door."

Ridley let the explanation hang there for a moment before turning his attention to the wider gathering.

"As I said, a difficult case to get to the bottom of… which is why I brought Lady Jane Scott on board to see if we could home in together on the killer."

Thirty-Five

Jane stood up and moved to the fireplace. All eyes tracked her.

"Well, here we are in this lovely old pub with its nostalgic oil paintings, horse brasses, and wagon wheels. I'm sorry we can't discuss the history of coaching inns today, but other things unfortunately demand our attention."

She took something from her pocket and held it up.

It glinted in the sunlight coming through the front windows.

"This is a gold coin. To historians, it's a Celtic stater. It was found in Rebecca Shaw's bag."

A bout of muttering flared up.

"The question is – how did it get there? For me, answering that question will identify Rebecca's killer, and Betty's killer too."

The muttering increased. Jane had to wait for it to subside.

"When we consider Rebecca's death, it's most likely she died close to where she was buried. The priory ruin is on private land. Why would a trespasser go up there to bury a body? There's too great a risk of being spotted."

"The Mortimers are free to come and go there," said Aubrey Enright. "It's their land."

"Yes, it is," said Jane. "But let's set aside the Mortimers for the moment."

She brandished the coin once more.

"Rebecca Shaw didn't dig at the site, and it's unlikely she simply found this while walking by. Such a coin would have been buried deep. The most likely explanation is that someone on the 1908 dig found it. But if so, how did it end up loose in Rebecca's bag?"

"There must be plenty of ways," said Jim Archer.

"No doubt it came from the Mortimer family," said Aubrey Enright. "They've had that land long enough to have found a coin. They must have given it to her to pay her off."

Teddy fumed openly.

"If that's so, why didn't I take the coin back? If it's valuable, why leave it with her?"

"Thank you," said Jane. "I considered whether the coin might have been discovered before the 1908 dig. Firstly, I wondered if Rebecca had owned it for a long time. A good luck charm, perhaps? But if that's so, why not mount it on a brooch or pendant?"

"What if she stole it from somewhere?" said Lavinia Mortimer.

"Then wouldn't she have sewn it into the hem of her coat or hid it in some other way? No, she didn't steal it. But if it wasn't theft, then what? Did someone give it to her? If so, it brings us back to the same question. Why have a valuable gold coin loose in your bag?"

Jane let her point resonate for a moment before pressing on.

"Let's keep with that idea. What if someone did give it to her? If so, when? If she received it in the days or weeks before her death, then, yet again, why have such a valuable object loose in her bag? Why not put it in her purse?"

"Quite so," said Kate, who sensed that Jane was getting to the heart of the matter.

"She might have feared robbery," said Sid Allen. "A thief might have taken her purse."

"A thief might have taken the bag," Jane countered. "After all, it contained other valuable possessions."

"Hmm…"

"So," said Jane, "let's imagine a scenario where she received it as a gift shortly before her death. A gift from her killer."

"That's fanciful!" said Aubrey. "Ridiculous, even. The killer would have taken it back."

Jane ignored him.

"Let's imagine it was put into her bag by the killer. A bribe, perhaps. But then she refused to comply. But, if so, as has been suggested, why let her keep the coin?"

Aubrey Enright rose to his feet.

"Inspector Ridley's evidence points to Teddy Mortimer. Why are we continuing with this nonsense?"

"Kindly hold your tongue, Mr Enright," said Ridley. "And sit down."

As Aubrey Enright did so, Jane drew a steadying breath.

"Betty Bagnall died at the hands of a murderer. But before she expired, her final act was to drag herself to her purse and retrieve a penny. Why?"

"I'll tell you why," said a firmly seated Aubrey. "The Mortimer family killed the governess to prevent blackmail. Then they killed Betty because she was going to tell you and your aunt what she knew. Betty tried to grab several pennies to represent the Mortimers, but in her weakened, confused and dying state she could only cling on to one."

"Yes, it's a compelling case, isn't it."

"I'm glad you think so."

"But we're examining an alternative that may yet prove even more convincing."

"Ha! More nonsense."

"Oh really? Then think on this, Mr Enright. What if Rebecca disturbed a trespasser? Someone who was around during the 1908 dig, and had discovered something, and covered it up. What if this person went back early the following morning when it was quiet."

"Why would you suggest that?" said Aubrey Enright.

"Because it explains everything – and I do mean *everything.*"

Thirty-Six

"How?" Aubrey gave a little laugh that he clearly hoped others would join in with.

"I'll come to that in a moment," said Jane.

"Who was the trespasser?" Teddy Mortimer demanded.

"Jim Archer," said Lavinia Mortimer.

"Rubbish!" said Jim.

"You killed your aunt because she knew you were responsible for Rebecca's death."

Ridley intervened. "Alright, let's not turn this into another punch-up. Lady Jane, please continue."

"Thank you, inspector. It's unlikely Jim Archer is Rebecca's killer. He wasn't on the 1908 dig. Therefore, it's unlikely he dug up an ancient coin."

Teddy shook his head. "I think we're reading too much into it. Perhaps the gold stater and the copper penny have no meaningful roles in all this."

"That would make perfect sense, except for one thing. Betty saw my drawing of the gold stater."

"So?"

"So, before that moment, she never asked to speak to my aunt and myself in private. I believe she thought the coin was important."

"Well… I suppose it's possible," said Teddy, somewhat grudgingly.

"The gold coin holds the answer," said Jane. "The question is how did it get into Rebecca's bag? What scenario can we come up with that answers that question without leaving room for doubt?"

"None," said Aubrey Enright.

"Oh really, Mr Enright?" said Jane. "What if Rebecca was offered more than one coin?"

"What?"

"What if our killer discovered a hoard of coins buried by monks to foil the King's men? And what if the presence of others nearby prevented a clean getaway? Might it be that this person covered the hoard and returned the next morning? How might that play out? Let's imagine Rebecca coming along early the following morning bound for Upton station… and discovering the trespasser at work… and reminding this individual that it's Lord Mortimer's land and therefore his treasure. What if this individual tried to buy Rebecca's silence? What if a handful of coins were forced on her, possibly even to the extent of being shoved into her bag? And what if honest Rebecca rooted them out and handed them back, but in that full bag, missed one?"

"Rubbish," said Aubrey Enright.

"Alright," said Jane. "Let's forget coins for a minute and consider scout badges."

Lavinia Mortimer rose to her feet. "I think Lady Jane's gone nuts and should be stopped."

"Yes," said Teddy. "Inspector, this has gone far enough."

Ridley remained impassive although perhaps somewhat less resolute.

But Jane soldiered on.

"Constable Drake kept his first scout badge. It's displayed on his mantlepiece. Why? Because it changed his life."

"How is that relevant?" asked Aubrey.

"Let's put all these factors together," said Jane. "Betty had seen a Celtic gold coin before."

"No, only your drawing," said Lord Mortimer.

"Yes, my drawing… which jogged a faded memory. I'm convinced she saw a coin just like it for real a long time ago. That's where Constable Drake's scout badge becomes important. He kept it as a memento of a life-changing moment… which made me think about other people who keep such mementos. I, myself keep a broken Victorian brooch I found when playing on a riverbank when I was eight. For me, it sparked my fascination with the past."

"This is getting us nowhere," said Aubrey.

"You're right, Mr Enright. Perhaps the landlord could assist us. Mr Jessup, we're talking about people who keep a trophy of something that changed their life. Have you ever done a similar thing?"

"Me?"

"Yes, you."

"I don't know what you're talking about."

"Now, that's just plain wrong, Mr Jessup. You know exactly what I'm talking about."

Thirty-Seven

All eyes were on Will Jessup, who – as far as Kate could tell – looked shocked to the core. For a moment, his powers of speech had deserted him. Jane meanwhile had a determined look about her.

"Back in 1908, someone got lucky. They had a lot of money come their way. Enough to buy an inn without requiring a loan, perhaps?"

"I told you – my second cousin helped me out."

"Mr Jessup, back in September 1908, when you were digging, you found something."

"No…"

"Celtic coins, most likely in a ceramic pot. We know there was more than one. But what if there were more than two? More than ten? More than a hundred?"

"None of this is true."

"You would have taken the pot with you. There's no way you could leave it there as evidence. Likewise, you couldn't risk burying the pot with Rebecca because, had she been discovered soon after, it would have suited you best for the investigator to assume death due to a random attack. The remains of a pot would have suggested that it once contained something. It was safer to remove it, which is what you did."

Will cleared his throat.

"No, this is all wrong. I'm innocent."

Jane turned to those seated around the first-class lounge.

"Put yourself in Will Jessup's shoes. Imagine... you've been called to the site to dig a number of trenches. It's late in the afternoon as you start on the last one, but they want it to be ready and waiting for them the following morning. You dig and dig... working up a sweat... and then... buried deep... a pot full of coins. You look up to where the archaeologists are across the field making their final efforts of the day. Do you shout to them in celebration? Or do you have a completely different thought? Yes, you do. At the bottom of your trench, you dig a deeper hole in the corner and you bury the treasure there in its new home. Now all you need do is get back there at first light and collect the treasure. The archaeology team won't be starting work for at least another hour or so after you've left with the loot. Only, that next morning, there's a woman coming along. Rebecca Shaw. She sees you. She surprises you. You try to bribe her. She refuses. If you're to keep the coins, you know what you must do."

"That's appalling," said Teddy Mortimer.

"It's not true," said Will. "None of it."

"You sold the coins, most probably in London, to create your cash fortune, but you couldn't resist keeping one as a memento of your life changing moment."

"I never had any fortune."

"It's how you bought the White Horse Inn."

"No, that was an arrangement with my second cousin. A sort of loan, as you've suggested. I paid him off years ago. Everyone in Penford knows the story. It's a well-known fact."

"Is it? Well, perhaps you can give Inspector Ridley your second cousin's home address, and also the paperwork relating to repayments and so on."

"What? No, he died."

"That's no problem – just give us his date of death."

Ridley nodded and took over.

"Constable Drake, take out your notebook. Mr Jessup's going to give you the details."

"Yes sir," said Drake, producing his book and pencil. "Ready when you are, Mr Jessup."

"I... I don't remember."

Ridley raised his eyes.

"I've met some liars in my time..."

"No..."

Jane took over again.

"Mr Jessup, are you denying that you kept a gold coin as a souvenir?"

"That's right. I don't have any gold coins. It's all lies."

"And yet when Betty saw my sketch of the coin, she decided that she wanted to see myself and my aunt to discuss an important matter. I believe she had seen a similar design long ago. Now, over the years, she worked in many places, both here in Penford and in Upton. But I believe it was here in the White Horse that she saw a coin just like the one in Rebecca's bag."

"Impossible," said Will. "I defy you to find one!"

"Well now, Mr Jessup, that's quite a challenge."

Thirty-Eight

Jane changed direction.

"Oh, by the way, I was sorry to hear of your horse brass falling down."

"What?"

"It's a three-foot-long, four-inch-wide, black leather strap studded with shiny brass embellishments – the kind that would decorate a shire or parade horse's harness gear on ceremonial occasions. They add an authentic touch to the inn's décor, but occasionally, those nailed into plaster fall down."

"Oh that? Yes, well… you're right about that. It's no bother though. Easy enough to nail up again."

Aubrey Enright stood up. "I'll tell you what *is* a bother. This business of Teddy Mortimer's cigar being found at the scene of Betty's murder."

"Yes, I agree," said Jane. "It's very troubling. Did you mention this to Teddy when he was sitting with you earlier?"

Aubrey seemed surprised.

"He wasn't sitting with me earlier!"

"He must have been. There's one of his cigar stubs on the floor by your foot."

"What?" Aubrey peered down to the offending item by his shoe.

"Unless someone placed it there earlier," said Jane. "We should never rule out such things in a murder investigation."

Aubrey fell silent.

"Now," Jane continued, "let me admit to you what a fool I was for much of this investigation. I overlooked something simple. Cause and effect. Betty Bagnall lived in Penford for sixty years without being murdered. Mr Jessup's horse brasses were undisturbed high up on the walls. Then Rebecca's body was discovered, Betty was killed, and a horse brass fell down."

"There's no connection," said Will.

"Cause and effect invites us to believe otherwise. Allow me to explain. The horse brasses are in the pub. Betty worked in the pub. Her final act was to get to her purse and take out a coin. Why? Because the coin is a crucial element. Oh, by the by, Mr Jessup, I forgot to mention that one of the archaeology students, Harry Gibson, was upstairs earlier. I asked him to keep an eye out for anything unusual. Harry?"

All turned to Harry, who was standing in the arch between the first-class and public saloons.

"I saw Mr Jessup go out with a watering can. He proceeded to water the roses."

"There's nothing unusual about that," Will protested. "It's warm weather."

But Harry wasn't finished.

"Between watering, he broke off to do something else, Jane. You asked me to keep a close eye on him. As far as I can tell, he dug something up by the rosebush in the far right-hand corner. Whatever it was, he put it in his waistcoat pocket."

Will Jessup looked worried.

"I don't understand."

"The horse brass," said Jane. "I suppose we get used to seeing them in pubs these days, but some are unique. By that, I mean the design of the brass plaques can be quite singular. Of course, they're tightly bound to the harness strap, which means a bit of effort to tamper with one. The strap that fell down was over the wall end of the bar. Its topmost brass fitting… a spoked wagon wheel with a black central circular hub that has a design of its own. I can't quite see it from here, but the hub seems to have disappeared."

"There's been some terrible misunderstanding," Will Jessup uttered.

"There was no business arrangement or loan from a second cousin," said Jane. "You already had enough money to change your life. You just needed a way to explain it. It would have taken a while to sell the coins – a few at a time, perhaps. It was a year or so after you found them that you bought the pub with the proceeds."

"I…" but Will Jessup couldn't finish the sentence.

"The horse brass was the key. The coin was painted black and mounted in the centre of the brass wagon wheel. Mr Jessup, for eighteen years, you took pleasure in hiding a trophy in plain view of everyone."

"No…"

"Betty told you that a coin just like yours had been found with Rebecca. Suddenly, you needed to silence her."

"No."

"You killed Betty and returned here as fast as possible to remove the coin from the horse brass."

"No, it's not true."

"I expect you were wondering what to do with the coin. You couldn't leave the pub again. You avoided suspicion by getting back fast and staying put. But where to hide it? In your room? Or somewhere else inside? No, if it were found, you'd become a main suspect. So, you got it as far away as you could while remaining here. Had anyone sought you, you would have appeared promptly."

"I don't think it's right to be questioned like this."

"Mr Jessup, you rehung the horse brass strap and buried the coin in the garden. Betty was a good worker. She polished the counter. And yet when my aunt and I came in, there was dust on it."

"Bad plaster, that's all."

"Dust on the counter and you returning from watering the plants in the garden. An interesting combination that gave me cause to wonder... and the beginnings of a theory. Your confidence in yourself was supreme, Mr Jessup. Supreme, but misplaced. If I was right, I just needed to find a way to scare you into digging the coin up again."

"No..."

"It must be burning a hole in your pocket. Constable Drake, if you wouldn't mind."

Drake strode up to Will Jessup and delved into his waistcoat pocket. He held up a black circular item.

Jane nodded.

"For almost two decades, that was the hub of a decorative brass wheel – a trophy displayed covertly to everyone who came in... you know what to do, Harry."

Drake handed the coin to Harry who was already holding a small penknife. He began to carefully scratch a little of the paint away.

He then held it up. "Gold!"

"Inspector Ridley, if you could match Will Jessup's coin to the one we found in Rebecca's bag."

Ridley did so.

"They're the same."

"What do you think of that, Mr Jessup?" asked Jane as she turned to the bar.

But Mr Jessup was no longer there.

Thirty-Nine

As one, they ran round to the other side of the bar and through the open staff door. The chase then took them out through a back door into the garden, and over the low fence.

Ridley detailed Constable Cartwright to grab the other Upton constable's bicycle and use the bridge past Mortimer Hall to get to the other side of the river. All the while, the rest were shouting for Will Jessup to stop. But he wouldn't listen.

By now, Kate had fallen back. She wasn't cut out for cross-country pursuit or indeed any kind of pursuit. Jane stayed with the leading pack though – as they followed their prey.

Will led them across a quarter of a mile of rough ground before he charged into the river. It came up to his knees but was fast flowing. He stumbled.

He raised himself again, but a puffing Constable Cartwright brought the bicycle to a halt at the top of the far bank.

The rest arrived out of breath, trapping the fugitive.

There was a stand-off, perhaps while Ridley assessed his options. This gave Kate the chance to belatedly join them.

"Come on…" gasped Ridley. "Out you come."

Will Jessup said nothing. He wouldn't move either.

"Drake, help him out."

Constable Drake stepped into the water, but Will Jessup took several steps away.

"How many coins were there?" Jane asked from the bank.

"Quite a few," said Will.

"How many did you try to give to Rebecca?"

He looked up the river and then downstream too, as if a way out might yet present itself.

Eventually, he turned to Jane.

"A handful. I tried to buy her off."

"But she refused."

"Yes, she refused. I'd just got lucky for the first time in my life, and I didn't want it taken away from me."

"What happened?"

"I held them out to her, but she waved them away – so I shoved them in her bag. She rooted around for them and threw them out again."

"Except she missed one."

"I didn't realise."

"You told her to forget what she'd seen, but she turned back to the hall."

"Yes."

"So, you hit her with a shovel."

Will declined to confirm it. "I told her we could both be rich."

Ridley sighed. "What about this second cousin?"

"Ha! All he had was a battered old cart selling second hand furniture."

"And Betty?"

"She was working for me back then. I always wondered if she'd caught a glimpse of the thing when I was painting it. Yesterday, she asked me about it…"

"Come on then, out of the water."

"I blame Teddy Mortimer," said Will, more passionately. "If it wasn't for his wrongdoing, Rebecca wouldn't have been passing that morning."

"That's not an excuse," said an exhausted Kate.

"It was easy enough to retrieve a cigar stub from the ashtray and plant it at the murder scene. Everyone else already thought he was a killer."

"Constable, get him out," said Ridley.

But a defeated Will Jessup stepped out unaided.

"For a while, I was the luckiest man in the world," he declared.

"William Jessup, I'm arresting you for the murders of Rebecca Shaw and Betty Bagnall. You don't have to say anything…"

"But I do. I'm not a bad person. It was the circumstances that did it. I wasn't greedy. I was torn about taking the coins. It was a case of should I…? Or shouldn't I…? I didn't know what to do, so I hid them again. It was a sleepless night while I worked up the courage to act. It was a cold sweat when I took my pick and shovel up there at first light…"

"We know the rest," asked Kate. "But why didn't you take your wealth elsewhere?"

"Fear! I was sure she'd be found. I mean the vicar was talking about another dig. If I'd left, it would have looked suspicious. No, I stayed. Then, by the time things settled down, I had the pub and a good life as a successful bachelor."

Ridley shook his head.

"Take him away, constable."

"Yes sir," said a wet Drake.

Ridley then turned to Kate and Jane.

"Well done. I can't claim credit for cracking this one."

"Neither can we," said Jane. "That goes to Betty Bagnall. She solved two murders."

Perry Nash then popped up.

"Look, this probably seems a bit strange, but we've found something."

Forty

Kate, Jane and Perry were walking to the priory.

"It's ironic," said Kate. "Will Jessup's fortune was a curse. Perry, you stayed at the White Horse Inn in 1908."

"I did and it was terrible. Under no circumstances would I have gone back there had it stayed the same. I'd have happily walked from Upton each day."

"But there was no need. Thanks to the ill-gotten money Will spent on it, the White Horse Inn lured us all there."

A short while later, there was a large gathering by the ruin.

"Just waiting for the inspector," said Perry.

"I was thinking of the White Horse," said Kate. "It's now a Mortimer asset, is it not? I mean it was bought with gold coins from the Mortimer Estate."

Lavinia smiled. "I expect it will bring in a good income. I certainly have some plans for the profits."

"Surely, once the paperwork's sorted out, it'll be owned by Lord Mortimer," said Jane.

"It's the same thing," said Lavinia.

"Who'll run it?" Kate wondered.

Ursula laughed. "Mother and Father?"

"Jim and Anne Archer," said Lord Mortimer. "They'll run it – if they'll accept."

Jim was suddenly beaming. "We will!"

"And you shall have a chance in life. Ten years free rent. I do hope you build a nest egg and use it wisely. You should have a very substantial deposit for a bank loan and I'll sign a legal option for you to buy the place if you're willing."

Jim and Anne Archer were beside themselves.

"We'll give it everything!" Anne declared.

Kate was delighted.

"Perhaps the Mortimers and Enrights will get together in the pub for a sing-along," she said.

"What about Uncle Aubrey?" Jane asked.

Aubrey, of course, was a notable absentee.

"He'll be too tired to come in," said Jim. "I mean being behind the grocery counter is bound to wear him out. Unless he can get someone in by paying decent wages."

Dennis Wells stepped forward and offered a hand. Jim shook it.

"Dennis, for you it's free beer… er, for a week or two."

Dennis smiled. And then laughed.

Just then, Aubrey Enright came bounding up.

"Uncle?" said Jim. "A change of heart?"

"It's something Lady Jane said. I just realised… this case would never have been solved without my vital role."

Everyone looked at him in disbelief.

"Don't you see? I scared off the killer which enabled dear Betty to alert us to the connection to the gold coin. I'm just glad to be part of bringing a murderer to justice."

Kate smiled and wondered how many weeks would pass before Aubrey had completely reinvented the entire episode with himself as the hero.

Next to come racing across the pasture was the vicar.

"I got here as fast as I could."

Lord Mortimer cut in.

"Good news for you, vicar. Two gold Celtic staters have been recovered from the 1908 dig. There's a bit of a process going on with them at the moment, but I'd like to donate them to the church fabric fund. I'm sure you'll be able to sell them for a good price."

"Oh, that's wonderful, Lord Mortimer. Thank you."

Finally, Ridley came up to join them, citing paperwork for the delay.

"Well," said Perry, "we found this."

He held up a small, purple, oval amethyst that bore an engraving.

"It's a 12th century Christ Pantocrator. Or, if you prefer, a rare icon from the East. The reverse is marked St Catherine, Sinai, where we know a certain prior spend time as a young man. Now, if you'll come this way…"

All arrived at a trench by the old medieval path. There were bones in the bottom of it.

Ridley frowned.

"I sincerely hope you're telling me that's five hundred years old."

Professor Nash solemnly shook his head. And then he brightened.

"More like six hundred, inspector. Judging by the items with the body, it looks like we've found Prior Wilfred."

A cheer went up.

Kate was thrilled for them all. It was a triumph. And she was especially pleased for Jane and Harry. They were good together with an ease in the way they interacted. It was early days yet, but they surely had a bright future together should they wish to pursue it. That was their business, of course. Kate's role was a simple one – to wish them all the very best and help in any way she could.

Just then, something came back to her. Lord Mortimer's words about the daughter he never had. Watching Jane, Kate understood it entirely.

She stepped aside from the throng and turned to the ruin. It had been a difficult few days, but they had come through it. She would return home fulfilled. And Jane would be coming to stay with her for a couple of days. Why then did it not feel perfect?

She thought of Perry. Hopefully, she would see him again.

In fact…

Be bold, be bold…

What to say though…? Perry, perhaps you'll visit Sandham at some point. I'd love to show you around. There's lots to see, history-wise.

There, she had said it – at least to herself. Now it was time to go straight up to Peregrine Nash and say it out loud… and see what he thought of it.

The End (Until Next Time…)

Don't miss the next book in the series:

"The Unfortunate Death of Lord Longbottom"

England, March 1929

In Aunt Kate and Lady Jane's fourth light-hearted cozy mystery, Lord Longbottom keels over during a party. It looks like he's been poisoned – but what do his dying words, "Sir Christopher!" actually mean?

Publication Date mid-2024

*

For details of all books by B. D. Churston, please visit the website.

www.churstonmysteries.com

Printed in Great Britain
by Amazon

37145530R00138